SAVING EVIE

BROTHERHOOD PROTECTORS WORLD

LK SHAW

Copyright © 2019, LK Shaw

This book is a work of fiction. Names, characters, places and incidents are products of the author's imagination or used fictitiously. Any resemblance to actual events, locales or persons living or dead is entirely coincidental.

© 2019 Twisted Page Press, LLC ALL RIGHTS RESERVED

No part of this book may be used, stored, reproduced or transmitted without written permission from the publisher except for brief quotations for review purposes as permitted by law.

This book is licensed for your personal enjoyment only. This book may not be re-sold or given away to other people. If you would like to share this book with another person, please purchase an additional copy for each recipient. If you're reading this book and did not purchase it, or it was not purchased for your use only, please purchase your own copy.

BROTHERHOOD PROTECTORS

ORIGINAL SERIES BY ELLE JAMES

Brotherhood Protectors Series
Montana SEAL (#1)
Bride Protector SEAL (#2)
Montana D-Force (#3)
Cowboy D-Force (#4)
Montana Ranger (#5)
Montana Dog Soldier (#6)
Montana SEAL Daddy (#7)
Montana Ranger's Wedding Vow (#8)
Montana SEAL Undercover Daddy (#9)
Cape Cod SEAL Rescue (#10)
Montana SEAL Friendly Fire (#11)
Montana SEAL's Mail-Order Bride (#12)
Montana Rescue (Sleeper SEAL)
Hot SEAL Salty Dog (SEALs in Paradise)
Brotherhood Protectors Vol 1

CHAPTER 1

THIRTEEN YEARS ago

"BUT DADDY, when will I see you again?" I choked the words through my tears in the courtroom, ten feet from my father. It was as close as my foster mother would let me get.

"Not for a long time, baby. But I promise I'll write, and I'll call you as often as I can. Now, I want you to be a good girl while I'm gone, okay? I want you to study hard. Keep up your grades so you can get into a good college. Make me proud, Evie."

I tore myself from June's grasp and raced to my father, to throw my arms around his waist.

"I love you, Evie."

He kissed the top of my head before June pulled me away from him. Tears streamed down my face as the sheriff's officer led my shackled father away to serve out his sentence.

"I love you, Daddy," I screamed just as the door closed behind the last view of his back.

CHAPTER 2

Eight years ago

"You're eighteen now, Evelyn. It's time for us to get married."

I stared in slack-jawed shock at the proclamation coming from my soon-to-be former foster brother, Stanley. Tomorrow was my eighteenth birthday, and I would no longer be a ward of the state. For five, wearisome years I'd lived with Robert and June Paulson, along with their son, Stanley and daughter, Vanessa. The latter had made my life miserable since the day I arrived at the Paulson's house. Stanley, on the other hand, took to me instantly.

For the most part, Robert and June had been

apathetic foster parents. All things considered, I could have wound up in a number of worse places, so for that, I was grateful. For the past six months, though, Stanley's affection had increased. Not that I expected to hear him say we should get married. Besides, I abhorred him. He'd been a weasely young man who'd grown into a weasely adult.

"Married?" My voice rose in pitch.

Stanley straightened to his not-so-impressive height and threw me an affronted glare. "You were meant to be my wife the minute you came to live with us. I thought you knew how I felt about you. I've been waiting all this time for you to grow up. You're mine, Evelyn."

Chills raced down my spine at his eery, obsessive tone. He'd been waiting for me? This was so not good.

"Stanley, I've told you a hundred times not to call me Evelyn. And sorry, but I'm not marrying you. I'm only eighteen. Besides, I don't love you."

A hint of darkness flashed behind his eyes, but when he blinked it disappeared. "I see. Well, perhaps while you're off at school, you'll realize how wrong you are. It's fine, Evelyn. I'll wait until you see reason."

Before I could respond, Stanley turned and walked out the front door.

"You think you're so much better than all of us, don't you?"

My head whipped around at the sneer in the female's voice. Vanessa stood in the doorframe, hatred oozing from her pores. I shook my head in confusion.

"What? No, I don't. Why would you even think that?"

Vanessa uncrossed her arms and closed the distance between us. She didn't stop until she'd moved into my personal space, close enough I could almost count the lashes around her eyes. I refused, however, to back down.

"You've had Stanley panting after you for years, leading him on, making him think he had a chance with you. I can't wait for you to leave. I hope I never see you again."

Without giving me a chance to reply, Vanessa followed in her brother's wake, leaving me standing there confused and irritated. She wasn't the only one glad I was getting out of here. Those two were bat-shit crazy.

CHAPTER 3

Present Day

I'd driven more than halfway across the country from Arlington, Virginia to Bitter Rock, Montana, and not once did I expect to show up to a two-story, run-down ranch house, left to me by an uncle I didn't even know I had. I also didn't expect this overwhelming rush of adrenaline. This buzz of energy. For the last three years, ever since my medical discharge from Delta Force, I'd been struggling to find a purpose. Apparently, taking on a dilapidated house and struggling ranch was it. The problem was, I had no idea what I was doing. Yes, I was capable of some of the repairs, but there were too many for just one person. And running a successful, or what I hoped would be a successful, ranch... Not a damn clue.

Figuring the repairs could wait another day, I needed to shift my focus on my other work. Work that actually paid my bills and had given me something to occupy my time since leaving the military. After almost tripping over the single loose step, I made it into the room I'd been using as an office for the last three days. I settled onto the office chair with its ripped upholstery and tilted to one side on the uneven wheeled legs, quickly righting myself with a curse. Once I was sure I wouldn't topple over, I fired up my computer. After several keystrokes, I was logged in and opening the file sent over by my former Delta-Force team leader, Tate "Bear" Parker. After glancing over the enclosed data, something wasn't adding up. I needed verbal, not digital, information so I picked up the phone.

"What can I do for you?" came the gruff greeting.

"Hello to you too, Bear."

"Ah, Nichols. To what do I owe the pleasure?"

"I got the file you sent, but I need some clarification on something."

We discussed the case he was working on and the

type of security check that needed to be done. Once we were on the same page, I went to work.

Almost six hours later, and after a quick lunch break, I shut down my computer and drove into town. I'd made a short list of items to pick up at the hardware store, and I needed to get there before they closed. The ranch was about ten miles from Bitter Rock itself. I took that time to look around me, and felt a surprising connection to this wild land.

I made my way down Main Street until I spotted Wells Hardware. I was standing in front of roof shingles, comparing different ones, when voices the next aisle over caught my attention.

"I'm a hard worker, dependable, and I never get sick. You won't be disappointed, I swear."

I heard the desperation in the man's voice.

"I ain't hirin' no ex-con. You might as well git," came the crusty reply.

A heavy sigh echoed in the otherwise quiet hardware store. "Thank you for your time anyway, sir."

A compulsion of some kind had me turning the corner to catch the man before he left.

"Excuse me? Sir?" I called out at the same time he reached the front door.

The man turned and glanced around like he

wasn't sure whom I was speaking to. I stuck my hand out. "Sebastian Nichols. And you are?"

Almost reluctantly, he took my outstretched hand and shook it. "Paul Vincent."

"What sort of job are you looking for?"

His expression dimmed even further at my question, but he powered through. "At this point, I'd take any honest work. Truthfully, there aren't a lot of things I'm qualified for, but I'm a hard worker and I learn quickly."

I studied him closely, taking his measure.

"Tell me what you were in for." I gave him credit for not flinching at my question, although he did straighten and push his shoulders back a little.

"Armed robbery." His answer was succinct.

"How long did you serve?"

"Twelve years. Been out for almost two."

"I may have some work for you." Running a background check on Mr. Vincent here was easy enough to do, considering my connections. I'd always been a good judge of character, and something told me there was more to this man than just being an ex-con.

He tilted his head, his skepticism showing.

"Daddy, wha—" A woman rounded the corner. She jerked to a halt and stopped mid-sentence.

Nothing about her appearance should have been noteworthy. Not her mousey brown hair, pulled back in a severe bun. Nor the pale, peach-colored blouse or the matching, boring peach and brown plaid, knee-length skirt she wore, which did more to accentuate her — size — than flatter it. Her chocolate-colored loafers were just as bland as the rest of her. Except her eyes. They were the bluest-green, like the waters off the coast of Belize. They pulled me deep into their depths, and I welcomed the drowning sensation. I was so captivated by their brightness, it took me a moment to realize she was speaking.

"— looking for you."

"Evie, sweetie, Mr. Nichols just offered me a job."

His sudden excitement was tangible. Her eyes darted to meet mine, and I sensed her confusion. "Mr. Nichols—" she started.

"Please, call me Sebastian."

"Mr. Nichols — Sebastian," she began again, blinking back tears. "I don't know what to say."

Her voice was husky and instantly I pictured sweaty, naked bodies rolling around on satin sheets. A small, unexpected, and highly unwelcome shiver raced through me. I was horrified that my cock twitched. I squashed the image faster than I could blink.

"You don't have to say anything. I have work that needs doing around the property, more work than I can do alone. Honestly, it's for purely selfish reasons I'm hiring him."

I pulled out my business card and handed it to Mr. Vincent. "Here's my information. Give me a call in the morning."

He took the card from me, clutching it like it was the most important piece of paper he'd ever touched. "Thank you. I promise you won't regret this."

I nodded. "I'll talk to you in the morning."

I'd just reached my car when I heard my name being called. I turned at the feminine voice and came face-to-face with Ms. Vincent. Arms crossed, I leaned against the car as she moved to stand close enough a waft of citrus circled around me. My nostrils flared at the scent. "I thought I told you to call me Sebastian."

Her face was in shadows, so I couldn't be sure, but it seemed like a blush crawled across her cheeks.

"Sebastian," she began again. "Why are you helping my father? Please don't get me wrong, I'm forever grateful. I'm just surprised."

I didn't know the answer myself. "As long as he works hard, there's no reason I shouldn't."

She studied me under the streetlight, perhaps trying to gauge my sincerity. "Well, I appreciate it more than I can say. You won't regret it."

"I'm sure I won't." I stepped away from my car and grasped the door handle. "Have a good night, Ms. Vincent."

I slid behind the steering wheel without waiting for a response. Something about this woman had me itching, and I needed to get out of here fast.

CHAPTER 4

I STOOD outside Wells Hardware for several minutes after the car disappeared down the road. Mr. Nichols —Sebastian— was absolutely gorgeous. When I'd rounded the corner and seen him standing next to my father, my breath had caught. The flecks of gray in his brushed back hair glinted like silver, and had my fingers twitching to touch it. His face was tanned and weather-worn. My gut told me the lines radiating from his eyes weren't from laughing. His matching salt-and-pepper scruff was neatly trimmed, and I had the sudden desire to know if it was as soft as it appeared.

The sound of a bell had me turn to see my father step out of the store, his eyes unfocused, and a silly grin on his face like he still couldn't believe what just happened. He gave his head a small shake, and his gaze landed on me.

"Two years I've been looking for someone to hire me, and boom. I think this is a sign that things are turning around for me, Evie, girl."

One would think after twelve years in prison my father would have turned jaded. Instead, it was like his time behind bars only made him more naive. After my time with the Paulson family, I found it hard not to be cynical. It was a good thing my father and I balanced each other out.

"You might be right, Daddy. I'm so excited for you. When you call Mr. Nichols in the morning, let me know what day and time he wants you to start work. I can drop you off on my way to the school."

He wrapped his arm around my shoulder and walked me down the sidewalk. "If not, I'll find a way to get there. Don't you worry about a thing."

I squeezed him back. "You know I always worry about you."

He kissed my temple. "I know you do, Evie girl."

We walked to my car and headed home. An hour later my father and I were sitting down to dinner.

"How are your lesson plans going for tomorrow?"

I set my fork down and wiped my mouth. "I'm

almost done. I didn't think it would be such a huge change moving from middle school to junior high, but good grief, these kids keep me on my toes."

My dad beamed with pride. "You're a wonderful teacher, Evie. Those kids are lucky to have you."

I sent him a smile and returned to my meal. "I'm really proud of you too, you know. I know how hard you've tried finding a job. I admire the fact that you've never given up."

That look of awe returned to his face, but then changed. He worried his lip. "I just hope I can do all the things Mr. Nichols needs for me to do. I'd hate to show up for work and figure out this was all for nothing."

I patted his hand. "You're going to do great. I have faith."

We finished dinner and cleaned up the kitchen together. I always enjoyed the time my father and I spent together, but there were moments when a surge of loneliness suddenly swept through me. Like tonight.

And when I crawled into bed, I tossed and turned the entire night, visions of Sebastian Nichols bouncing inside my head.

CHAPTER 5

THE RUMBLE of tires over gravel traveled through the open window above the kitchen sink. I glanced out to see an older model Oldsmobile pull up the driveway. The passenger door opened and Paul Vincent exited the car. He looked back and waved at his daughter, who sent him an encouraging thumbs up. I watched until her car reached the end of the drive, almost disappointed she hadn't gotten out to say hi.

"Morning," I greeted him. "Come on in."

"Good morning," He brushed past me with a bright smile.

"Can I get you some coffee?"

I walked back into the kitchen with him on my heels.

"No, thank you. I had my cup-a-day limit already."

I sent Paul a mock appalled look. "How can you survive on only a cup of coffee a day? Have a seat."

He slid into a chair, and after pouring myself another cup, I followed suit. "I didn't drink coffee for twelve years. Now, if I drink more than a cup, it makes me jittery. I could probably get away with decaf, but Evie buys the strong stuff, so I make do with my single dose."

I shook my head. "I'm not even approachable until after my second cup. Anyway, I made a list of things I want to try and tackle today."

I rose and grabbed the slip of paper I'd left by the coffee pot. After returning to where Paul sat, I laid it in front of him to look over.

He glanced up at me. "I'm gonna be honest here. The stairs, gutters, and roofing, I think I can manage. But I know nothing about repairing a chicken coop."

I sent him a reassuring smile. "You're in good company then, because neither do I. What I do have, though, is access to the internet and endless video tutorials."

Paul almost visibly sagged in relief. "Thank god. I was nervous you'd send me packing on my first day."

I patted him on the shoulder. "You have nothing to worry about. Everything will be fine. Do you mind if I ask you a few personal questions?"

He nodded. "You're my boss. It's only fair you know what you're getting into."

"What did you do before you got sent away?"

He threaded his fingers together on top of the table. "I worked two jobs actually. Believe it or not, I was a schoolteacher. I also drove a city bus in the evenings."

How the hell did this guy go from teacher to armed robber?

"My wife died giving birth to Evie. Hemorrhaged. Suddenly, there I was, a single dad and recent college grad, at the age of twenty-four. I did the best I could, but it only seemed like things got harder and harder, especially the older Evie got. Even with two jobs, I was struggling to make ends meet. One night, I just hit a breaking point. It was like some other person inhabited my body. The next thing I know, I'm holding a gun and robbing a convenience store."

Paul paused, his eyes unfocused as though reliving his past. He shook his head and glanced over at me, his head high and shoulders back, just like at the hardware store. Daring me to respond.

"You only wanted what was best for your daughter."

"I still do. Evie could have written me off. I mean I was gone a long time. But she didn't. She wrote to me every week. Never missed a letter. Then, the day I got out, she was there to pick me up."

For a moment, I envied him for having that kind of love and loyalty from someone. As if this damn unsettling attraction I felt for Evelyn Vincent couldn't have gotten worse.

"So, that's my story."

I dipped my chin. "Thank you for telling me. Now, why don't we get started?"

"That's it?"

I paused from rising from my seat with a questioning glance. "What do you mean?"

"You hire a stranger, an ex-con, practically sight unseen. I tell you I robbed a store with a gun, and you just shrug it off and say let's get to work?" He narrowed his eyes. "Maybe I should be the one who's worried."

"I don't think either of us have anything to be worried about. I work for a personal protection agency owned by another former military member. My expertise happens to be in computer technology and security. I researched you the minute you told me your name. I knew most of what you'd already told me. I just wanted to hear you tell it."

"I didn't realize."

I shrugged him off. "You seemed like a guy who needed a break. I can't do everything around here by myself. It was a win-win situation for both of us. Now are you ready to get to work?"

Hours later, I stood on the rooftop, wiping sweat from my forehead with my discarded shirt when the sound of tires on gravel reached me. "Paul, your daughter is here."

I descended the ladder and my foot had just hit the ground when Evie pulled to a stop. Paul waved at her from the roof, and she returned the gesture. Without giving it a thought, I strode toward her, throwing my shirt over my shoulder. She rolled down the window at my approach.

"You have a great father there."

Her eyes darted past me and settled on her dad for a brief moment, a smile gracing her face, before returning to me again. "Thank you, yes, I do."

Paul reached the car just then. "I put away the tools I used, Mr. Nichols. Same time tomorrow?"

I raised an eyebrow. "I'll have you calling me Sebastian before we're through. And yes, same time tomorrow."

He waved and hopped into the car. I took a step back and raised my hand in farewell, my eyes landing on Evie and remaining there. She flushed and rolled her window back up before switching gears, making a k-turn, and heading down the driveway. I stood there for several minutes before heading inside, my thoughts continuously drifting to Evelyn Vincent.

CHAPTER 6

I'D BARELY KEPT from swallowing my tongue when a shirtless Sebastian had approached. It had taken every ounce of willpower not to let my gaze drift down his lightly furred chest and follow every bump and ridge of those washboard abs. My mouth almost started watering just picturing that single bead of sweat that dripped off his chin and landed with a splat onto his sternum. I'd quickly averted my gaze before getting caught.

"How was your first day?" I asked my father to distract myself from all that naked flesh.

"Oh, Evie, it was actually one of the best days ever. Don't get me wrong, it was hard work, but the chance to do something truly productive after all this time? It was more than I could ask for."

"I'm so happy for you, Daddy."

He turned toward me. "What about you? How was school?"

I couldn't help but sigh. "It was great for the most part. Except there's one girl..."

"Yes, what about her?"

"I think she's getting bullied, but I can't prove it. I caught her crying in the girl's bathroom after lunch, but when I tried to talk to her, she shut me out. I brought it up to the principal, but there didn't seem to be a lot of support from that end. I just don't know what to do."

"Sweetie, sometimes there isn't anything you can do, but keep being there for her. Let her know that she can trust you and that you're there to help."

I glanced over at him. "Is that what you did?"

A wistful expression crossed his face. "It's what I tried to do."

I spent the rest of the drive thinking about what my father said. Once we arrived home, I quickly changed clothes before putting dinner in the oven. I'd just sat down to relax when my cellphone rang.

"Hello?"

"Hey, Evie, it's Shelby Davis."

"Hi." I tried to sound natural when, in reality, I was wondering why she was calling me. We chatted often in the teacher's lounge, but I wouldn't call us friends.

"I'm sorry to call so late, but a few of us are getting together after school tomorrow, and I wanted to see if you'd like to come. We're meeting at Donahue's for dinner and some drinks at six."

To say I was surprised was an understatement.

"Let me check with my father, but I think I should be able to make it."

"Fabulous. Well, I'll see you in the morning."

"Yeah, see you."

After disconnecting the call, I stood there just staring at my phone while I smiled a little stupidly.

"What has you looking all giddy?"

I startled at my father's question and looked up to see him enter the kitchen and check the food in the oven.

"That was one of my co-workers. She invited me to go out with them after school tomorrow."

"That's fantastic sweetheart. I'm so happy you're starting to make friends. I know it's been tough for you with me hanging around."

I pulled back and scolded him. "You stop that right now. I love being with you."

He brushed my hair back. ""I just feel like I've held you back these last two years since I've been out. During that time, you've never been out on a date and this is the first time you've gone out with friends. I worry about you. I don't want you to let opportunities slip by because of me. You're a grown woman. Live your life. I'm okay. I promise. I want you to go out with your friends. Enjoy your time with them. Understand?"

I studied him. "I understand."

He pressed a kiss to my forehead. "Good. Now, is this food ready? Because I'm starving."

I laughed when he smiled at me. "Almost. I'll call you when it's done."

My father turned and exited the kitchen again. I sat down at the table and pulled out my book to read for a bit. I'd just finished the next chapter when my phone rang again. "Hello?"

Static sounded on the other end of the line.

"Hello?" I asked again.

Still no response.

"I can't hear you. If you can hear me, you'll need to call back."

I'd just pulled the phone from my ear to disconnect when a guttural voice sounded.

"Bitch."

"Excuse me? Who is this? Hello?"

Nothing but silence. When I glanced at my

phone, it had returned to the home screen and the call was disconnected.

A shudder crawled down my spine. Was that really meant for me, or did someone dial the wrong number? Either way, it creeped me out.

CHAPTER 7

IT HAD BEEN another long day of repairs. Paul hadn't lied when he'd told me how hard he would work. He got more accomplished than I did. Especially when I had to take a two-hour break to work on a project for Bear. After Evie had come to pick up her father, I thought about throwing a frozen dinner in the microwave, but I jumped in the car and headed into town. An ice cold beer or two sounded good right about now.

I pulled into Donahue's and cut the engine before heading inside. Before long, I was taking a long draw from a cold bottle. Directly in front of me was a mirror and I studied the reflections of people coming and going. I'd always been a people watcher, wondering about their lives and how they all took for granted the things around them. I'd just taken another pull from my beer when I paused mid-swallow, set the bottle down, and turned.

Standing just inside the entryway of the restaurant was Evie. For two days, I'd spent every minute pointedly not thinking about Evie Vincent. I didn't think of her sapphire eyes. Nor did I think of the soft swell of her belly or the rounded curve of her hips. I definitely didn't picture her heart-shaped ass under that unflattering brown skirt she'd worn at the hardware store.

She waved at someone I couldn't see and walked through the restaurant. I was struck by how…curvy and lush she was. Her black skirt dipped in at the waist before flaring out over her hips. Her royal blue shirt was tucked in and only served to highlight her generous curves.

Somehow, I knew she had thick thighs. The kind you could sink your fingers into when you're thrusting deep inside her. I had no interest in the woman. But, damn if I couldn't stop thinking about her.

Who was she here with? Was she on a date? Pissed that my curiosity was getting the better of me, I threw my napkin on my plate and pushed away from the bar. I headed through the restaurant, telling myself I was just going to use the men's room.

Finally, I spotted her sitting at a table with three other women. They all looked like they were having a good time. I hurried into the washroom, and when I came out, I almost collided with a soft body. I reached out to steady the woman.

"Oh, I'm so sorry."

"Evie?"

Blue eyes peered up at me. "Mr. Nichols? What are you doing here?"

"I was having dinner. What about you? And stop calling me Mr. Nichols. You make me feel old," I scolded her like the crotchety old man I refuted being. It was then I realized I hadn't let go of her arms, and I dropped my hands like I'd burned them. She flushed.

"I'm just out with some co-workers." She gestured over her shoulder.

I followed her gaze, even though I'd already seen them, and then returned my eyes back to her. "Looks like you ladies are having a good time. I'll let you get back to it. Have a good night."

"Yeah, you too."

I walked away from her and drove home. My foot caught on the still-loose step halfway up the staircase, and I cursed as I tripped and almost landed face first before catching myself on the railing. After safely making it the rest of the way upstairs, I plodded into my room and sat on the edge of the bed. I pulled up my pant leg, pressed the button on the side of my prosthetic, and the whoosh of air releasing sounded as I pulled it off my stump. I rolled down my liner and rubbed the aching end of what was left of my leg.

I knew I'd overdone it the last couple days, but there were so many things I needed to get done around this place.

I opened the drawer of the nightstand and pulled out the object stored inside. My finger traced a path across the face of the beautiful woman behind the glass. She was trying to hold onto her wild and wind-blown blonde hair, all the while laughing hysterically, her hazel eyes dancing with mischief. I'd lost so much three years ago.

My leg.

My career.

My wife.

I tried to think of what my life would be like now if she were still alive. Instead, blonde hair morphed into brown, and hazel eyes shifted to bright blue-green. Her form filled out and lush curves replaced the previous slim figure. I shifted uncomfortably on the edge of the bed. Not only from arousal, but from the guilt.

The two women were the exact opposite in every way. Natalie had been tall and leggy, with laughing eyes and blonde hair. A spark of life followed everywhere she went. Evie, on the other hand, was short and curvy. Her eyes were, more often than not, serious and solemn. Regardless, something about her had me sitting up and taking notice. Some part I'd thought long buried.

Apparently, my defense mechanism to keep my distance from her was to be a jackass. With a final glance at the picture, I pulled open the nightstand drawer and tucked the frame away. Natalie was gone, and she wasn't coming back.

I grabbed the pair of crutches I kept by my bed and hopped into the bathroom, pulled the container of Epsom salt out from under the sink, and while the hot water ran, I dumped half the carton in.

While the tub filled, I shucked my clothes, and with a hiss, I lowered myself into the steaming water. I reclined back and attempted to relax my stiff muscles. Eventually, only a dull ache remained. Usually I was able to clear my mind while I soaked, but tonight my brain wasn't having any of that shit.

Instead, it raced with the image of a woman. A groan rumbled out of my chest as I pictured her stepping into the tub with me, her siren's body naked and water dripping off the tips of her beaded nipples. I licked my lips at the thought of tasting the berry red buds.

Unconsciously, my hand drifted through the water and closed around my now-hard cock. Another groan escaped as I began stroking my length, squeezing it the way I liked. The water aided my effort as my strokes grew faster. I sucked in several breaths and imagined it was Evie's pussy clenching down on me. With just another few jerks of my hand, I came, gasping out her name on an exhale.

I laid there until the water cooled. Then, I pulled the plug and dragged myself upright. I turned on the shower and rinsed my body off before clumsily getting out of the tub and drying off. I hopped to my bed and pulled back the covers before collapsing in an exhausted heap. Before long, I was fast asleep.

CHAPTER 8

My father had been working for Sebastian for just over a week now. Every day was the same. I'd drop him off and pick him up at the same time. Unlike that first day, though, when he'd walked over to the car, Sebastian never spoke to me. In fact, he barely even acknowledged me. I got the impression he didn't like me.

My ego was a little bruised.

I shoved away all thoughts of Sebastian and focused on finishing up my grocery list. Early Saturday mornings was when I did all my shopping. Already it was getting later than I liked. I quickly scanned my list and added some more vegetables to it. I tried to make sure we ate healthy. Otherwise, my butt, hips, and thighs suffered the consequences.

An hour later, I was scurrying down the aisles of the Save-More. I rounded the corner on my way to the check-out when I clipped the front end of another cart with mine.

"The fuck?" The expletive was definitely from a male.

"Oh my god, I'm so sorry."

My eyes connected with none other than the man I'd avoiding thinking about.

"Evie." He said my name in a tone I couldn't decipher.

"Good morning. Sorry about the fender bender there." I smiled good-naturedly, trying to make a joke about our collision. My smile wasn't returned. In fact, it seemed to only make him frown even more. Well then. I stiffened my shoulders and maneuvered around his cart.

"Anyway, sorry."

I hadn't made it five steps before I stopped. Screw this. I turned to face his back.

"Have I done something to offend you?" The words popped out of my mouth.

Sebastian pivoted and we now stood face to face. I continued when he remained silent.

"I've obviously done something. Every morning I

drop my father off and every evening I pick him up. I try to be friendly, but clearly I've offended you in some way, because all I get are frowns and glares. So, whatever it is, I apologize."

"There's nothing to apologize for Ms. Vincent."

"I see. Have a good day then, Mr. Nichols," I replied stiffly and turned back to my shopping cart to make my way to the checkout.

"Evie, wait."

Ignoring the plea, I kept moving.

"Damn it, Evie, stop."

Nope, not doing it.

"Evelyn Vincent, don't take one more step."

I stopped and slowly turned. "I don't think we have much more to say to each other. Regardless of what you say, it's obvious you don't like me for some reason. I think it would be best if we didn't speak in the future."

Sebastian held up his hands in surrender. "I'm sorry, okay. I know I've been a jerk."

I snorted at the understatement.

"I deserve that. Truly, I am sorry for making you think you did something wrong. You didn't do anything. I also apologize for being rude and unfriendly. I don't have any excuse."

He continued standing there with a forlorn look on his face. I didn't doubt his sincerity. Cursing at myself, I caved.

"Fine, apology accepted."

He inclined his head. "Thank you."

I crossed my arms over my chest. "Just so you know, I'm still pissed. And I don't think I like you."

Sebastian's gaze darted down before quickly returning to my face. "Fair enough."

Now that there didn't seem to be anything else to say, I needed to get out of here. "See you around."

"Bye, Evie." He looked like he wanted to say more, but seemed to change his mind.

~

I WAS HOME PUTTING the groceries away when my father entered the kitchen.

"You okay, hon?"

I tossed a head of lettuce with more force than necessary into the crisper drawer before turning to face him.

"Of course, why?"

His lip quirked up. "Maybe because you seem really angry with that poor vegetation."

I huffed out a breath of air and collapsed against

the counter. "I might have gotten into a small argument with Sebastian at the grocery story."

He pulled back in surprise. "Sebastian Nichols? Whatever for?"

"It was stupid really."

My father gestured toward the table. "Sit."

Knowing it was pointless to argue, I took a seat. He laid his forearms on the surface and linked his fingers. "Now, tell me what happened."

Replaying the altercation in my head had me groaning internally. I totally over-reacted. I dropped my forehead briefly on the table before sitting back.

"I accidentally ran into his shopping cart. Then I basically accused him of being unfriendly to me, and I demanded to know why. And now I feel like an idiot. This is why I don't have any friends. I'm socially inept."

"Evelyn Elise Vincent, I don't want to hear you talk like that," my father scolded.

"It's true," I whined. "I had to make a huge deal out of him not talking to me, instead of just ignoring it and moving on with my life."

"Oh, Evie."

I stood from the table. "I'm sorry, Daddy, but I don't feel very well. I'm going to my room."

I left the kitchen and headed upstairs. Not caring

that it was barely noon, I crawled into bed feeling sorry for myself. I don't know how long I laid there replaying the entire confrontation with Sebastian, but eventually I drifted off to sleep.

CHAPTER 9

I NEEDED to make it up to her, starting today. Heading downstairs, I went into the kitchen to brew a pot of coffee. I'd just taken my first sip when I heard the familiar sound of tires coming up the drive. Stepping out onto the front porch, I gave a short wave at the car's approach. Like every day for the past week, the father and daughter briefly conversed before Paul exited the vehicle. I walked over to greet him.

"Morning, Paul."

"Sebastian." Finally, after a week, the man says my name, although I detected a slight reproach in it. He and Evie must have had a little chat about our run in on Saturday. I was curious what she told him.

I was thankful though for the warm weather, because I noticed her window was down.

"Morning, Evie," I called out.

Almost reluctantly, I think, she raised her hand in acknowledgment and returned my greeting.

"Bye, Daddy." She put the car in reverse.

"Bye, Sebastian," she added in an almost trying-to-be-polite afterthought.

I remained standing there until her car disappeared. Turning my head at the sound of a throat clearing, my eyes landed on Paul, who I'd completely forgotten about.

"So, want to tell me what's going on between you and my daughter?"

Honestly, I wasn't sure where to start.

"Let's go inside."

He followed me into the kitchen where I reheated my coffee. I gestured for him to have a seat.

"I joined the Army fresh out of high school. I busted my ass in training and eventually became a Ranger. It wasn't until I was a Ranger for five years that a man approached me asking if I'd like to try out for a special, covert unit."

"Delta Force."

I nodded. "Three years ago, we were on a hostage rescue mission in Iraq. Two American journalists had been captured. We entered the town, located the hostages, and began extraction. Only, it was a trap. During the crossfire, one of my buddies was wounded. While I was dragging him to cover, the town was hit with a rocket launcher. Buried under rubble for days, I was presumed dead."

Paul's eyes were wide with horror. "Holy shit."

I ignored his exclamation.

"While I lay there, almost bleeding out from having my leg blown off, back here in the States, my wife was killed by a drunk driver."

"Jesus, Sebastian, I'm so sorry."

I waved him off. "It was a long time ago."

"Still, I know what it's like to lose your wife. Your soul mate. It's something you never recover from."

I studied him. "Is that why you never remarried? Sorry, that's a little personal."

Paul waved me off. "No, no, it's fine. That's part of it. I loved Elise more than anything. We were high school sweethearts. You know, the typical cliche. But the instant I saw her there was a spark. One I wanted to be around."

"That was Natalie. She was so vivacious and full of life."

"So you know what I mean. After Elise died, I spent all my time taking care of Evie. There wasn't time to date, even if I wanted to. And then prison happened. You don't meet a lot of eligible women in there."

He winked at me, and I couldn't help but chuckle. "No, I guess you don't."

Paul's forehead wrinkled. "I still don't know what any of this has to do with my daughter."

I shifted awkwardly in my chair. This was Evie's father. It felt like the time I picked up my senior prom date and her dad looked at me like he just knew I was about to corrupt his beloved daughter.

"I'm"—I coughed to stall for time—"attracted to your daughter, sir."

His expression lit up like and then turned sympathetic. "Ah, I see. And you're not too happy about it, I take it?"

I scoffed. "Not particularly."

"I understand now why she thinks you've been prickly to her."

Almost laughing, I smothered the smile. "Prickly is putting it nicely." I shrugged.

"Anyway, I guess that's what's going on between me and your daughter."

Paul sighed. "I did a huge disservice to Evie when I went away. I encouraged her to focus on her studies and get good grades, when I should have been encouraging her to make friends and have fun. To do all the things a little girl should do when she's growing up. Instead, she took my words to heart. She studied harder than any of her classmates and she graduated at the top of her class. She's an amazing teacher. But she's also had trouble connecting with people. It might have to do with the foster home she grew up in. She doesn't talk about it much, but I know she didn't have it good there. Just one more sin I have to live with."

I filed that little bit of information away. It never occurred to me to wonder where Evie had grown up while Paul was in prison.

"You obviously did the best you could for her at the time. And now you two are together and able to re-form that father-daughter bond."

"I guess. But I do have one question for you."

That made me nervous. "What would that be?"

"What are you going to do about your feelings for my Evie?"

CHAPTER 10

"No, no, no. C'mon, don't do this to me" I begged while smoke curled and rose from under the hood. "Please."

I pulled off the road into the grass, and the car sputtered and died, gasping out its last breath. "Damn it."

My cell phone lay buried at the bottom of my purse, so it took a minute to retrieve it. Finally, I snatched it and my wallet.

"My car just died, and I need a tow, please." I spoke to the road side assistance operator on the other end of the line. I tried to patiently answer all her questions about what kind of car I drove, and who my insurance company was, when suddenly her question was cut off mid-sentence.

"Hello? Are you there?" I glanced at the phone and cursed.

My phone was dead. My head dropped back against the headrest. I wanted to cry. This day could not get any worse.

Someone pounded on the window, and I screeched like a pissed-off owl.

Mother fu— I guess this day *could* get worse. I shoved the door open, almost knocking over the man standing in the way.

"You"—I paused trying to think of an appropriate name—"asshole. Were you trying to give me a heart attack?"

I exited the car, my tone rising three decibels with each word I shouted at Sebastian, and slammed the door behind me.

He held his hands up in surrender, backing away from my verbal attack. "Whoa, sorry. I didn't mean to scare you. Everything okay?"

I waved my hand in the direction of my Oldsmobile, still smoking behind us. "Does that look like everything is okay?"

Sebastian studied the scene like a detective solving a crime. "It appears you're having some car trouble."

I threw my hands up disgust and huffed away, mumbling several obscenities under my breath.

"Damn, Evie, I didn't realize you were that easy to rile. Do you mind if I take a peek? Maybe I can figure out what the problem is."

I gestured an invitation with my hand. "Feel free."

"Can you pop the hood for me, please?" he asked, standing at the front of the vehicle that still belched out smoke.

I re-opened the door, pulled the lever, and then stepped around to where he stood, my eyes following the length of his arms, his muscles flexing and contracting with each movement. Even his fingers had my attention as he searched for the cause.

"Have you been leaking oil?"

It took me a moment to realize he was speaking. "Not that I know of."

He turned his head, peering at me over his shoulder. "Do you actually check your oil level? This is an old car, and it's possible you have a leak. Unless you're doing it consistently, you'd never know."

Considering the tone in Sebastian's voice, he clearly thought I was an idiot. I wanted to roll my eyes, but refrained.

"Yes, I check the oil. Every time I pull the stick

out, there's oil on it. So, I don't think that has anything to do with it."

He blinked, and the expression he shot me had me uncomfortable.

"You do wipe off the dipstick, slide it back in and back out, and then see if there's oil on it when you check it, right? Please tell me you do that."

Suddenly, my whole body grew warm, my cheeks especially. Because apparently I was an idiot.

"No one, not even the mechanic who changes the oil, ever showed me that. My college roommate just told me to pull the yellow ring and the stick would come out. If there was oil on it, then I was fine. I didn't know there was more to it. God, I feel so stupid."

My emotions were getting the best of me, and to my mortification, tears threatened. My throat closed, and I swallowed multiple times while I willed the liquid in my eyes away. There was no way I was crying over something as dumb as this in front of Sebastian. Honestly, I couldn't believe he hadn't already made some sarcastic asshole comment.

"Hey, these things happen sometimes. Here let me show you. Do you have a napkin or tissue in your glovebox?" His question was surprisingly gentle.

Pulling myself together, I hurried to the passenger side and grabbed a napkin.

"Here." I held it out to him.

"Come closer, so you can see what I'm doing." He gestured with his head at the same time he grabbed the yellow-ringed handle and pulled out the dipstick.

"First, you wipe all the oil off so you have a clean stick going in. Then, you slide it back down, pull it out, and see where your oil line is." He spoke while he demonstrated each step. "Oh, yeah, look at this." His blunt-nailed fingertip pointed to the end of the metal stick. "There's almost no oil on here. Which means you've run out. It's possible you cracked a head gasket, which could account for all the smoke."

"So, what does a cracked head gasket mean? I'm going to guess it's not something inexpensive."

"I'm afraid not. You're probably going to need to have the entire engine replaced. Depending on the year of the vehicle, you might be able to find one at a repo or junk yard that won't cost you an arm and a leg. But that means you'll have to head to Bozeman. Your chances of finding anything around here are gonna be slim to none, I'd wager."

I stepped back and sighed in defeat. What was I going to do?

"Son of a bitch."

After shutting the hood, Sebastian turned and leaned against it. "I can make some calls for you if you'd like. Not sure how much good it will do, but I can see if the owner of Redd's Garage can order one in for you. That is, if that's what it needs. I'm not a mechanic or a car expert so you're gonna have to get it to a shop. Do you have roadside service?"

"I was talking with them before you banged on the window, but my phone battery died mid-call."

He shifted toward me, pulling his phone out of his back pocket. "Here, use mine. Once you get your car towed, I'll give you a ride home. It's getting dark out and there's a storm heading this way."

I hesitated. I wasn't even sure I liked him, but I was definitely attracted to him.

Even his scent was intoxicating. It made me want to nuzzle his neck and follow the delicious aroma wherever it led. Damn this stupid attraction.

"Oh, sorry, I'd appreciate the use of your phone and a ride. I'll just be a minute."

Our fingers brushed when I plucked the phone from his hand and the heat from his skin sizzled its way up my arm, down my body, and straight to my core. It was unreal how strongly I was affected by the barest of touches.

Forty minutes later, the tow truck pulled up and the driver loaded my car up. He was given the address to Redd's Garage, and after he'd driven off, Sebastian turned to me.

"You ready?"

Not in the slightest. "Thanks for giving me a lift. I really do appreciate it," I said after I'd pulled myself up into his older model truck and buckled up.

The second he smiled at me, my brain short-circuited. Two perfect dimples appeared on each side of his mouth, and every rational thought flew out of my head.

CHAPTER 11

"It's my pleasure."

When I first saw the smoking car pull off onto the side of the road, I had no idea who was behind the wheel. I'd gotten an almost perverse pleasure from startling the prissy school teacher when I pounded on the window. Imagine my surprise when that Valkyrie emerged. She'd been pissed and not afraid to tell me off.

"Why are you being so nice to me?" Evie asked after several minutes of only the sounds of Steely Dan coming from the speakers.

I winced at her question.

"You looked like you needed a friend back there."

"Isn't that the sad truth? Do you know I've been living in Bitter Rock for almost two years, and I don't have a single friend? God, how pathetic is that? It's even more pathetic that I'm telling you,"

I darted a quick glance in her direction to see her resting her temple against her fist as she stared out the passenger window, watching the trees whoosh by. She seemed so utterly lonely, and that resonated deep inside me. It had me examining my own life and lack of people in it.

Not choosing to think it through, I found myself laying my hand on top of hers. She startled at the contact and turned her head swiftly in my direction.

"If it makes you feel better, I don't really have any friends either," I said softly.

I turned my head and my gaze flitted toward her for just a moment and unspoken words passed between us. Then, she smiled and winked. "Yeah, but you're also kind of an asshole."

I burst out laughing. "There is that."

Neither of us said anything more for a few minutes. It was a comfortable silence, but I found myself wanting to fill it anyway. I wanted to know more about this lonely woman next to me.

"So, what brought you to Bitter Rock, anyway?"

Evie didn't respond right away as though weighing her answer before speaking. "We, my dad and I, needed some place new to start over. When I saw the job listing for a teacher, I applied, and —" she shrugged "—here I am."

Her answer seemed too simple. "How old were you when your dad went to prison?"

My eyes remained on the road, but I saw her flinch. "Twelve."

From what I learned from her father, he'd spent the same amount of time in prison. Add the two years they'd been living here and that made her twenty-six. Over a decade separated us.

"Where'd you live while your father was in prison?"

"What's with the twenty questions all the sudden?" she asked defensively.

Not that I could blame her. I was being terribly intrusive, but I just couldn't help myself. Now that I'd acknowledged the attraction, I wanted to know more about Evie Vincent.

"I'm curious, is all. Passing the time." I tried to sound nonchalant, like it didn't matter if she answered or not.

"Well, for every question I answer, you have to do the same. And you're one question behind."

"Fine. What's your question?"

"Why'd you really hire my father? After that first

day at your house, you knew he wasn't going to be able to do half the things you needed done."

It was my turn to be surprised. Of all the questions, I hadn't expected that one. I took my time answering.

"Because he was your father."

Her nose scrunched. "I don't understand."

Keeping my eyes averted, I continued. "Because I know what it's like to have to start your life over. To feel like the world's against you. I've always rooted for the underdog."

Evie seemed confused by my answer. "Why don't you like me?"

"Is that your next question?"

She shot me a dirty look. "Yes."

"I'm attracted to you, Evie. Besides, I've never said I didn't like you. So, where did you live while your father was in prison?"

"Wait a minute. What do you mean you're attracted to me? And, no that's not my next question, but you're going to answer it anyway." She glared at me.

I pulled over, put the truck in park, and unbuckled my seatbelt. I slid across the bench seat until our thighs touched, reached out, and palmed the back of her neck. Slowly, giving her a chance to stop what was happening, I lowered my mouth, stopping millimeters from hers. Evie's chest quickly rose and fell, and just as I finally completed the connection between us, her breath hitched.

The kiss was tentative at first, but when I nipped her bottom lip, she opened on a gasp. Taking advantage, I slipped my tongue inside, getting my first full taste of Evelyn Vincent. She tasted of strawberries, my favorite fruit. When she moaned, I caught the sound. It had been a long time since a simple kiss affected me this quickly. I shifted to try and ease the ache behind my zipper, but it only made it worse. Especially when Evie's hand landed high on my thigh. Our tongues continued their dance until, eventually, I pulled back slightly.

Her eyes remained closed and her lips glistened with wetness. We were both breathing hard.

"That's what I mean by being attracted to you."

CHAPTER 12

Holy cow. Sebastian kissed like he'd been abandoned in the Sahara and I was the first water hole he'd come across. He drank from me like his thirst would never be quenched.

How do you go from not even liking someone to wanting to rip all their clothes off?

The plain and hard truth was, I was a twenty-six year old virgin. I'd been so focused on my studies and making my dad proud that I never spent much time on anything but my grades. I was also a little self-conscious about my body. I'd dated some in college, but there hadn't been that sizzle with any of them. Sure, I'd fooled around, but when it had come time to seal the deal, I couldn't follow through.

With Sebastian, I was surprised the sizzle hadn't

scorched me alive. My whole body felt like it was on fire. Nerves had anxiety racing through me. I wasn't cut out for this kind of thing.

"You okay?"

I startled at the sound of Sebastian's voice. "Oh, yeah, I'm fine. Why?"

"You looked kind of like you were about to have a seizure over there, and I wasn't sure I if I needed to pull over again."

Oh god.

Then, he burst out laughing, and I knew he'd been messing with me.

"You're such a jerk."

Sebastian's laughter subsided. "I'm sorry, Evie. You just had this terrified expression on your face. It's not a big deal, you know. We're attracted to each other, and we kissed. It doesn't have to be any more than that."

I threw him the stink-eye. "How do you know I'm attracted to you? Yeah, I might have let you maul me, but that doesn't mean anything."

He didn't say anything as he finally pulled into my driveway. He parked the truck and, without unbuckling his belt, turned toward me, his intense stare making me twitchy.

"You can call that kiss we shared whatever you

want to, but don't lie to yourself. We both know you enjoyed it and this attraction between us is mutual." Sebastian's expression was fierce and unforgiving.

"You're right." I swallowed hard and twisted my hands in my lap. "I'm sorry. This is just new to me, and I didn't know how to react."

His gaze softened a little. "What do you mean new to you? Surely that wasn't your first kiss? You're twenty-six years old."

Oh god. Please, lightning, strike me dead now.

I hastily unbuckled my belt. "You know what, never mind. Thanks for the ride."

I dove out of the truck as the skies opened and the rain began. Just as I'd reached the front door, a soaking wet Sebastian grasped my arm to stay any further movement.

"Hey, what happened back there? Talk to me, Evie."

Even while rain poured down our faces, my wet hair plastered to my head, the man in front of me still looked breathtakingly gorgeous.

"What do you want from me, Sebastian?" I asked in desperate wonder. Everything about this guy confused me. He was attracted to me and kissed like he would drown without another taste, yet he didn't even like me. He'd been rude, then jokingly gave me a hard time, then went out of his way to be nice and helpful. It was enough to make anybody crazy.

I could tell my question puzzled him because he took his time answering.

We stared at each other for a minute, neither speaking, until finally, he sent me a sad smile. "I don't want anything from you, Evie."

Before I could even respond, he walked away.

CHAPTER 13

THE PORCH SWING creaked and groaned under my weight, and it sounded overly loud in the early morning light. The smell of freshly brewed coffee filled my nose while I watched the sun crest the horizon. I'd slept like shit last night and had been up for almost an hour already thinking about yesterday. Evelyn Vincent was a distraction I didn't need. She confused the hell out of me with her mix of siren and innocence. That kiss though. I'd been rock hard within seconds of our lips connecting.

I couldn't stop thinking of Evie's soft lips. In the shower, I stroked my cock, gripping it hard the way I liked. Stroke after stroke, my breathing increased until I was panting. I rested my head on my forearm against the shower wall to hold myself steady as my balls tightened, and I moaned out Evie's name while my cock spit and the falling water washed my seed down the drain. Out of breath, I finished washing up before throwing on a pair of sweats and firing up the computer. Too keyed up to sleep, I tried getting some work done. Except, I couldn't concentrate on that either.

Evie's question played on repeat in my head. What did I want from her? It was a question, eight hours later, I still didn't have an answer for.

"Morning, Sebastian." Paul greeted me when he walked through the door, wiping his feet.

I hadn't heard any car pull up. Shit, Evie's car was in the shop.

"Paul," I said his name questioningly. "How did you get here?"

"I had a buddy drop me off." I could tell he was lying.

I stared him down like I had the young soldiers serving under me when I'd been a Ranger, sending him my most intimidating glare. He didn't even flinch.

"Well, since you're here, I have a ton of eggs and bacon left over. Why don't I grab you a plate and we can sit and talk for a minute before we get started."

I could tell he wanted to say no, but he nodded his head. "Thanks, breakfast sounds great."

As I plated our food, Paul took one of the island bar stools. "I should be finished with the chicken coop by tomorrow, and then I can get started on the fence line on the southeast corner of the property, if that works for you."

"Sounds good. Let me know when you're ready and I'll be out there to help. I have no idea what I'm doing. I may be wasting my time completely with everything else if getting the barn fixed is out of my budget."

Just then, the phone rang.

"Hello?"

"Sebastian, it's Evie. Did my father make it there okay?"

I glanced over at the man in question. "Yes, he's here."

"Good. Let him know I'll be picking him up this afternoon, and that he better not dare try to walk home."

"Excuse me?" I roared.

Paul shifted guiltily on his seat.

"Wait. He didn't tell you?"

"No. He said he got a ride from a friend."

Evie sighed heavily. "My dad and I are a lot alike

in the friendship area. We really only have each other."

For some reason, this made me incredibly sad and angry. "Well, now you two have me."

There was a long pause over the phone. "Thank you, Sebastian. That really means a lot."

"You're welcome. I'll let him know."

"See you this evening."

"Later," I replied absently as my razor-sharp stare zeroed in on Paul.

I pressed the end button and far too calmly set the phone down. I crossed my arms and my ankles and leaned back against the laminate counter top.

"Jesus, Paul, it's ten fucking miles from town."

Paul straightened his shoulders. "I know how far it is."

I slid back into my chair and rubbed my forehead. "Why didn't you call me? I would have given you the time off until Evie's car was fixed. Or I could have come and picked you up."

"I told you when you hired me that I was dependable. I made a commitment to you and I had every intention of keeping it."

Shaking my head, I slumped in my chair. "Tomorrow, I'm coming to pick you up if Evie's vehicle isn't repaired yet."

When Paul opened his mouth, I halted whatever it was he planned on saying. "End of discussion."

He snapped his mouth shut. "Fine."

"When you're done eating, we'll get to work."

~

A HORN HONKED and Paul and I looked up from the post we'd been placing into the ground. I didn't recognize the vehicle. We both stood, and I wiped my dirt-covered palms on my jeans as the car rolled to a stop by the house. I shaded my eyes as the passenger door opened and out stepped Evie.

"Hey," she called out.

Paul waved at her and signaled we'd be just a minute.

"Let's finish getting this post secured."

Apparently I'd been demoted from being the boss.

He cleared his throat. "I mean…"

I waved him off. "I know what you meant."

We quickly finished packing the dirt around the wood and making sure that it was firmly secured in the ground. We'd finish the rest in the next couple days. Side by side, we strode across the property toward the house and driveway where Evie and her ride waited. The closer I got, the clearer I could make out the driver. I recognized her as one of the women from the restaurant that night.

Paul strode past me and headed straight to his daughter for a hug. She returned the gesture, but it was clear she wasn't happy with her father. Her eyes met mine but then she broke contact.

"Evie." I inclined my head.

"Hi," she replied still not looking me in the eye.

"I told your father that I'd pick him up for work tomorrow if your car wasn't fixed yet."

"Thank you. I appreciate it. I talked to the shop today and it looks like the new engine should be in by the end of the week."

"No problem. Since I'm already going to be stopping at your house, do you need a ride to work? I don't mind."

Evie glanced at her friend behind the steering wheel, and I could tell she was weighing her decision. I knew when she'd made it, because her shoulders straightened. Exactly like her father.

"I'd appreciate it. Thank you." Evie's question returned inside my head, first as a whisper, then growing louder. What did I want with her? I headed upstairs, already knowing what the answer was. I just didn't know if I was ready.

CHAPTER 14

It was obvious Shelby had sensed the tension between my father and me yesterday, and I was glad she hadn't asked questions. When she'd dropped us off, I'd thanked her for the ride and gone inside without a word to my dad. He'd set off, on foot no less, on a busy road for ten miles without telling me. What if he'd been hit by a semi-truck or a car? One that didn't stop? He could have been lying in a ditch, dying, between here and Sebastian's house and I'd never have known. My father was the only person I had left in my life. So, yes, I was furious. And hurt. Both of which he sensed, because he didn't attempt to talk to me again for the rest of the night.

I'd fixed dinner, but taken mine to my room to eat. I'd woken this morning still upset, but my temper had definitely cooled. I understood why he'd done it. My father had always been a proud man. Which was why he hadn't asked for help all those years ago when he was struggling. Now, I stood in the kitchen making breakfast when I heard him step into the room.

"You talking to me today?" he asked warily.

I looked over my shoulder. "Maybe."

"I'm sorry I upset you."

I went back to cooking. "I know you are."

He approached my side. "Can I help?"

I shooed him away. "Go sit. It's almost done."

Before he turned around, he pressed a kiss to the side of my head.

Grabbing the spatula, I plated our eggs and bacon. We sat and ate, infrequently breaking the silence. Once the kitchen was cleaned up, my father peeked at the clock to check the time.

"I better go grab my umbrella. They were talking about storms today."

He hadn't been gone a minute when the doorbell rang. I hurried to answer it. On the other side of the door stood Sebastian, looking ridiculously gorgeous.

"Morning, Evie."

"Morning. Come on in. My dad just went to get his umbrella. He should be out in a minute."

After stepping over the threshold, he turned to me.

"Good, that gives me a minute to talk to you."

"Sure, what about?"

"I'd like to take you to dinner."

I certainly hadn't been expecting that.

"That would be nice."

Sebastian smiled. "How about tomorrow night?"

"Okay," I replied.

I was saved from any further discussion when my dad appeared.

We climbed into the pickup with me sandwiched between the two men. I could feel the heat of Sebastian's thigh against mine. Thankfully, the ride didn't last long and soon we arrived at the school. I hurriedly slid out of the cab and kissed my father goodbye. I waved at Sebastian and headed inside.

Shelby greeted me the minute I stepped inside. "Oh, good, I'm glad you made it. Okay so you have to dish. Who was the hunk from yesterday and this morning?"

It felt weird to have this… friendship suddenly. It was nice though.

"His name is Sebastian Nichols. My father works for him."

She sighed dreamily. "He's delicious. And completely into you."

I flushed at her words, remembering the kiss he and I shared. "No. We're just friends."

Shelby flashed me a look. "Honey, I don't know what planet you're living on, because that man wants more than friendship from you."

The bell interrupted any more conversation, and we both fled to our classrooms. For the rest of the day I thought about her words. Around five, his truck pulled into the parking lot, and my palms grew sweaty. Especially when I noticed he was alone. Sebastian pulled to a stop in front of me.

His smile was bright when our eyes met. "Hi there."

"Hi." I walked around the front of the truck and slid inside. "Where's my father?"

"I dropped him off already."

"Why?"

"So I could do this." Before I could guess his intent, he pulled me in for a kiss.

I sighed against his mouth. A woman could get used to this. The kiss lasted for several minutes before he finally severed our connection. I had trouble catching my breath.

"I've been waiting all day to do that. We're still on for dinner tomorrow night, right?"

"Hmm? Oh, yes."

"Good," he responded before putting the truck in drive.

When we arrived at the house I shared with my father, Sebastian pulled me in for another kiss.

"I'll see you in the morning?" he mumbled against my lips.

"Uh huh." I obviously couldn't form words.

Sebastian winked at me. "Have a good night, Evie."

"Oh, yeah, you too." I jumped down from the cab of the truck and threw a wave over my shoulder. "Thanks for the ride."

I scurried inside, a silly smile on my face and excitement for tomorrow night coursing through me.

CHAPTER 15

The end of the school day bell rang, and I quickly started tossing my things into my bag. A knock on my door interrupted me. I looked up to see Shelby standing in the doorway.

"Hey, the girls and I are going to Donahue's again tonight. What do you say?"

"Um, I can't tonight."

Her eyes lit up. "Oooh, a hot date?"

I felt the heat creep into my cheeks.

She clapped her hands in excitement. "Oh my god, you're going out with the hottie, aren't you? See, I told you he was into you."

"It's just dinner." I finished putting away my books.

"Doesn't matter. It's still a date."

I hadn't been on a date since college, and even then I didn't remember this level of anticipation. "Evie, breathe."

I heard the words and realized I was clutching my bag to my chest and breathing heavily. Immediately, I slowed my breaths down. Now I remembered why I didn't date.

She took my hands. "Relax. Just have fun."

I nodded, feeling foolish for overreacting. "You're right. It's just been a while since I've been on a date. I'm being silly."

"It's okay to be a little nervous. I remember my first date with Ryan. My nerves were so shot I could barely eat. In fact, I almost passed out, because I hadn't eaten all day. In the end, it all worked out. We've been together for three years now. It's going to be fine." She gave my hands a reassuring squeeze.

So this was what it was like to have a girlfriend. It was nice.

"Thanks, Shelby."

"You're welcome. Now, don't do anything I wouldn't do."

"Ha ha. Very funny."

I glanced at my watch. "Crap, I have to go. Sebastian should be here to pick me up."

"You're going to have a great time. I want to hear all about it tomorrow."

I hugged her.

"Thanks for everything."

"That's what friends are for. Now, get going, and I'll see you tomorrow."

I waved. "Bye."

Hurriedly, I rushed down the hall and stumbled outside. Sure enough, there on the other side of the parking lot was Sebastian's truck. And leaning against the driver's side door with a small bouquet was the man in question. Slowing my steps to avoid seeming overeager, I made my way over to him.

"Hi."

"Hello yourself." He held out the flowers. "These are for you."

"Thank you so much. They're beautiful."

"You're welcome. You ready?"

"I am."

We rode in silence for a bit, and I realized I didn't really know anything about him. I was curious about everything.

"How long have you lived in Bitter Rock?"

"I've only been here for about a month."

Sebastian's answer took me by surprise. "Oh

wow. For some reason I thought you'd been here longer."

He shook his head. "Nope. I'm actually from Virginia. I got a call a couple months ago from the executor of my uncle's estate telling me I'd inherited his ranch. Some uncle I didn't even know I had."

"My goodness. I imagine that was quite the surprise."

Sebastian chuffed. "You're telling me. Especially when I showed up to discover it was basically falling down."

"Is that why you were at the hardware store the night you hired my father?" I inquired once we were seated.

"It was. I'd gone to pick up some roof shingles when I heard Paul talking to the owner. Something told me to intervene. Which was a good thing, because your dad has been a godsend. I've gotten far more accomplished around the ranch than I expected I would. Especially with my bum leg."

I was confused. "What do you mean?"

Sebastian turned slightly in his chair, stuck his leg out, and leaned down to partially lift his pant leg. I leaned to the side of the table. I never would have guessed he wore a prosthesis. My gaze darted up to meet his, and I sensed he was waiting for my reaction. I sat back up while he lowered his pant leg and returned upright.

"I'm so sorry you were hurt."

He shrugged like it was no big deal. "It was a long time ago."

I reached for his hand. "Still, I'm sorry for the pain you suffered."

"Thanks. Anyway, it was my lucky day when I ran across Paul."

"I think we were the lucky ones," I said softly.

Our food soon arrived and we spent the rest of the evening talking. I could tell Sebastian was mildly uncomfortable exposing himself like he had, but I was glad he did. It meant he was human. I also wondered if that was the reason he'd been so aloof. Like maybe I would think less of him.

"What are you thinking about right now?"

I startled at the question and my gaze darted to Sebastian. I hadn't even realized I'd zoned out. Then my brain processed his question. How in the world did I answer him?

"Honestly, I was thinking how grateful I am you're a real human."

"A real human, huh? I suppose I should take that as a compliment."

I flushed. "That didn't come out quite right. This

probably won't either. You seem too perfect. Well, now that you're not being an asshole."

Sebastian threw his head back in laughter. "You're never going to let me live that down, are you?"

"Not a chance. But that isn't just it. You're good looking. Like some saint, you swoop in and hire an ex-con to work for you. It's like you don't have any flaws. Makes us mere mortals a little self-conscious about our own imperfections."

"I know what it's like to fight against insecurities, and it bothers me to think I've given the impression I think I'm better than anyone. If I've done that to you, and it would seem I have, I'm sorry."

There was a short awkward silence following that. I needed to say something to move us past it.

"Do you think you'll stay in Bitter Rock after your repairs and renovations are done? Or will you head back to Virginia?"

Sebastian leaned back in his chair. "I haven't thought too much about it. There is so much to putting the ranch back in order. Things I don't know a single thing about. Like cattle. There are a few hundred head still grazing in the pasture and being taken care of by a couple of men who worked for my uncle. They've been doing it for free since he died, but it's taking a toll."

"Have you talked to any of your neighbors? I'm sure they'd be willing to offer help or advice. That's one thing I've discovered about living in Montana. The people here are friendly and more often than not are willing to lend a hand to other ranchers."

He chuckled. "I wouldn't consider myself a rancher. Not even close. Hell, when I first got here, I almost turned around and high-tailed it back to Arlington. Now, I'm really glad I didn't."

His glance heated when his eyes locked with mine.

"Me too." We'd gotten off to a rocky start, but things seemed to be looking up.

"Do you know why I was always such a jerk to you?" Sebastian asked softly.

I wasn't sure if he wanted me to answer, or if the question was rhetorical. Apparently it was the latter, because he didn't give me time to respond.

"I used to be married."

I could feel a small kernel of jealousy roll around inside me.

"What happened?" Curiosity made me ask, even though I wasn't sure I wanted to hear the answer.

"While I was deployed, Natalie was killed in a car accident. She was seven months pregnant."

I gasped. "Oh my god, Sebastian. I'm so sorry."

He ignored my words. "Nat was the love of my life. When she died, I wanted to die too. Even though it's been three years, I still miss her every day."

Sebastian paused in reflection like he was thinking about his wife again. I tried to stop the bitter jealousy over a dead woman from forming, stop the hurt piercing my heart at hearing him say how much he loved his wife. It was difficult. God, I was a horrible person.

I was so engrossed in my own self-pity I almost missed what he said next.

"Then you came around the corner wearing that hideous brown skirt and ugly blouse. There shouldn't have been anything about you that made me look twice, but there was. Maybe it was some spark in your eye. Whatever it was, it was there, and I didn't like it. I felt disloyal to Nat and our marriage by being attracted to you. And I took it out on you by being an asshole."

Sebastian's gaze homed in on mine from across the candlelit table and everyone around us disappeared.

"I don't know where this thing between us is going, but I wanted you to know I am sorry."

I ignored the pang in my chest; the one that said I was falling for him. Rationally, I knew I confusing feelings of lust for something deeper, but I couldn't seem to stop them. Instead, I took his apology for what it was and prayed that my heartache wouldn't be great when this, whatever it was between Sebastian and me, ended.

CHAPTER 16

When we'd finished our dinner, I wasn't ready for the evening to end, so we went back to my place. Evie took one end of the couch and I took the other.

"Your dad tells me you grew up in foster care."

She sipped her beer and shifted. "I'm not sure how much my father told you."

"Just that your mother died, and you were in foster care while he was in prison. He said you don't talk much about it."

Her expression clouded. "My dad raised me all on his own until I was twelve. Then one day the police knocked on the door."

She paused and took another drink. "The next thing I know, I'm living with virtual strangers. Robert and June weren't true foster parents, just temporary guardians; some type of step relation to my mom's great-aunt. Honestly, I'm not even sure where the connection is. Not that it matters. That's where I spent the next five years of my life. I lived with people who weren't my parents. Two kids who weren't my siblings. They didn't treat me badly. They just didn't love me like my dad did."

Evie's whole demeanor changed while she told her story. I'd seen her spitting mad, nervous, and extremely happy. It was the first time I'd seen her eyes lack some kind of life. I scooted over and pulled her against my side.

"I don't think anyone can love us like our dads. It sounds like you had a shit childhood, and for that I'm sorry. What I see, though, is a strong woman. One who survived tough times and came out all the better for it. I know Paul is beyond proud of you. He tells me all the time."

She sank into me and I loved the feel of her soft body. "I missed him so much while he was gone. I try not to feel sorry for myself, but sometimes it was hard. Vanessa, the Paulson's daughter, hated me, and to this day I have no idea why. Then there was Stanley."

Evie shuddered. "He always gave me the creeps.

Following me around. God, when I was eighteen he told me we were going to get married."

I drew back in puzzlement. "He proposed?"

She shook her head and let out an unamused chuckle. "That was no proposal. It was a proclamation. When I told him I wasn't marrying him, he didn't take it well."

An innate suspicious feeling reared up inside me. "What was his response?"

"He told me I'd change my mind, and he would wait until I did."

"Where's Stanley now?"

She shrugged one shoulder. "I have no idea. When I first went away to school he'd make random appearances on campus, like he was reminding me of his presence. A letter here or there. A picture. He even sent me flowers when I graduated from college. But after my dad and I moved here two years ago, everything stopped."

Every protective instinct inside me flared. Someone didn't just suddenly stop stalking a person, and this Stanley guy had most definitely been stalking Evie. I made a mental note to run a security check on him as soon as possible. Until then, I decided I didn't want to talk about Evie's past anymore. I'd much rather focus on the present. I took the beer from her and set it on the floor at our feet. "I'm going to kiss you now, okay?"

"Okay," she whispered.

I leaned in and lightly brushed my lips against hers. Evie sighed against my mouth, and I breathed it in before deepening our connection. She opened beneath me, and I took her cue to dart my tongue inside to fully taste her. The breathy sounds she made hardened my cock even further. I continued learning her flavor and savoring it. She pulled back slightly and gasped in a breath. There was a glazed look in her eyes.

"Wow," she breathed out.

I couldn't help but smile and perk up with pride. "I assume that's a good wow."

She nodded emphatically. "Most definitely."

Then suddenly she seemed a little unsure of herself.

"What's going on in that head of yours?"

"I've never really done this before." She didn't make eye contact with me.

"What do you mean?"

Evie looked decidedly ill at ease when she gestured between us. "This. Dinner dates followed by going home with a guy. Making out on a couch. Any of this."

My eyes widened. "Evie… are you a virgin?"

"Is it that obvious?"

"What? No," I rushed to reassure her. "I'm just surprised is all."

She scooted back the short distance the end of the couch allowed her and crossed her arms over her chest defensively.

"I didn't really have any friends when I was in high school or college. My roommate was always partying, but I'd promised my dad that I would study really hard. So I did. I stayed in my room, did my homework, and graduated at the top of my class. There wasn't time for anything else in my life."

I hated that she'd withdrawn into herself. "There's nothing wrong with that. You had goals, and nothing was going to stand in your way of achieving them. I admire your determination."

Evie sent me a look that said she didn't believe me. "You don't think it's weird I'm a twenty-six year old virgin?"

"Unusual? Maybe. Although, I bet you'd be surprised by the number of women who wait. But weird? Definitely not."

She sat for several minutes not saying anything. "Do you think you could kiss me again?"

"I think I could be persuaded."

Her tongue darted out to wet her lips, and I groaned at the sight. I slid my fingers through her hair, gently guiding her toward me. We met in the middle, and I tilted my head before brushing my mouth across hers. I did it again and this time my tongue swiped across her lips, pulling in her flavor. She parted for me and I plunged my tongue inside hers for a fuller taste. She was sweet like berries.

Our tongues danced and tangled. Evie's tiny whimpers were music to my ears. I pulled back slightly to gasp in air, and our breaths mingled together. Then I dove back in. She met me kiss for kiss and clutched at my arms, her nails biting into my skin, the slight sting sending a zing of pleasure straight to my cock.

My free hand roamed from the place it had found at her waist upward until it settled right below Evie's breast, my thumb just barely caressing the underside of it. When she pressed herself even harder against me, I brushed across the nipple, feeling it pebble at my touch. She moaned into my mouth and swallowed the sound. Then she spoke against my lips.

"Do that again, please?"

CHAPTER 17

I'D BEEN MORTIFIED when Sebastian guessed I was a virgin. But the way he touched me, I quickly forgot about my embarrassment. Apparently I wasn't above begging either.

"Do that again, please?"

His thumb continued to caress the same spot below my breast, not moving any further in one direction or another.

"Do what?" Sebastian asked in a teasing tone.

"Stop being dense."

His chest rumbled with laughter. "Oh, you mean this?"

I sucked in air when his whole palm engulfed my breast and he began to knead it. I sagged against him in pleasure while he molded my flesh, my nipple pebbling even more beneath his palm.

"Yes," I hissed in pleasure.

That was the last word I said for several minutes because Sebastian's lips were covering mine again. I met his tongue with a flick of mine, and I pressed myself closer.

I didn't want any of this to end.

Suddenly, there was a huge crash outside and Sebastian and I broke apart. "Stay here," he commanded before jumping off the couch and darting toward the front door, his gait only slightly awkward and unsteady.

"I think some animal knocked over the trash barrel and it rolled down the gravel drive. I found it at the bottom near the road. To be sure, I took a quick survey around the barn and house, but nothing else seemed out of place."

I wanted to continue where we'd left off, but the mood had been shattered.

"Well, I'm glad it was only an animal. It scared the hell out of me."

Sebastian pulled me into his side and kissed my temple. "I guess I should probably take you home."

Reluctantly I agreed.

We were both quiet on the ride into town, but once we were parked in the driveway, he pulled me into his arms for a good night kiss.

"Come on, I'll walk you to the door."

We kissed a final time before I headed inside. I collapsed against the closed door with a happy sigh.

I almost danced through the house. Up until our startling interruption, tonight had been fantastic. I was falling for Sebastian. It wasn't his handsome face, although that certainly didn't hurt. It was the softness buried way down deep under his crusty exterior. It was the little things like apologizing for how he'd treated me. For hiring an ex-con just because he was my father. There were so many facets to his personality that, combined, made him irresistible.

When I reached my bedroom I turned on the light and headed for the bathroom to get ready for bed. I stopped in my tracks. There, on my pillow, lay a rose in full bloom and a piece of paper folded in half. I didn't even realize I was shaking until I reached down to pick up the note. I was transported back to college when I'd find notes from Stanley. This couldn't be from him, though. He had no idea where my father and I were.

Still, I made my way through the entire house, checking every window and door to ensure they were all locked. Once I'd double-checked they were all secure, I headed back to my room and fell into bed. I jumped at the sound of my phone. It rang several times before I answered it.

"Hell—hello," my voice came out shaky.

"I'm sorry, were you asleep already?"

My entire body relaxed. "No, I wasn't asleep yet."

"What's wrong? Evie, honey, are you okay?" Sebastian's voice was tight with concern.

"Nothing, it's fine. I'm okay."

"You don't sound like everything is fine. Talk to me, Evie." There was a command in his voice now.

"After you dropped me off, I came upstairs and there was a rose and note on my pillow. It probably came from my dad. I freaked out over nothing."

"What?" Sebastian roared. "Have you checked the house? Made sure all the locks are engaged? What about Paul? Is he okay? What did the note say?"

"Everything's locked and my dad is asleep in his room. Nothing seems out of place except for the flower and note that just said 'Thinking of you.'"

"I'm coming over."

"No, it's fine. I'm fine."

Sebastian growled. "You didn't sound 'fine' when you answered the phone, Evie."

I sighed. "Okay, yeah, I was a little freaked out, but all the doors are locked and there's no one here."

"You sounded more than spooked, Evie. Terrified is more like it. When Paul wakes up tomorrow, if he didn't leave it, we're going to the police. If someone was in your house, they have to know about it."

I nervously laughed. "I'm sure it was from my dad, and I'm making way too big deal about this."

"Evie," Sebastian warned. "Find out. Then, if need be, police. Understand?"

Reluctantly, I gave in. "I understand."

"Good. Now try and get some sleep. If you need me, you call."

I nodded, even though he couldn't see me. "I will. Oh, wait, did you need something?"

"No, I only wanted to hear your voice again. But now I'm glad I did. I don't have a good feeling about this, especially after the chaos at my house."

I agreed with him, but maybe if I ignored the sensation, it would go away.

"Morning, daddy." I sat next to him on the couch. "Do you have a minute?"

"Of course. Is everything okay? You don't look well."

My stomach turned over because I was afraid of his answer. "Did you leave a note and a flower in my room last night?"

His forehead crinkled in confusion. "Was I supposed to?"

My heart pumped and the ache grew in my belly. "I found them on my pillow last night."

"You're saying you found a note and a flower in your room last night?"

I didn't want to say the words out loud so I only nodded. My dad shot to his feet, almost spilling his coffee in the process.

"Dear god Evelyn, why didn't you wake me up when you found them?"

My hands gripped my thighs. "Because I was really hoping you had put them there."

He ran one hand through his hair in a combination of exasperation and fear while the other rested on his hip and he began to pace. "What did the note say?"

I cleared the gravel from my throat. "It said 'thinking of you.'"

"Christ. We're calling the police."

He stepped over to the phone and dialed the number before I could even think to stop him. Not that I would have, because Sebastian was right.

I needed to call him.

"Evie, are you okay?" was his greeting.

I wrapped an arm around myself. "I'm fine. My dad is on the phone with the police."

There were muffled curses coming from his end of the line before his voice came across clear. "Are they coming to the house?"

Back and forth I paced. "I don't know. He's just now on the phone with them."

"I'm staying on the line until you find out."

"Wait, he's off the phone now." I held the phone away from my ear when my dad turned to me.

"The police are on their way over. What did you do with the things?"

I pointed upstairs. "They're in my bathroom trash."

"Good. We'll leave them there."

I returned to Sebastian.

"I heard. I'm on my way into town now. I'll be there soon." I was glad he was coming. "Thank you."

"You don't have to thank me. I'll see you soon."

"Okay."

There was no response and I knew he'd ended the call already. Now all I could do was wait. I didn't want to sit outside with my dad, so instead, I sat on the end of the couch and pulled my knees to my chest.

CHAPTER 18

I HIT speed dial the minute I got off the phone with Evie. Bear answered just as I jumped into my truck.

"What can I do for you, Nichols?"

Not wanting to waste any time, I dove right in. "I have a situation and might need some back-up over here in Bitter Rock. There was a break-in at my... friend's house last night while she wasn't home. Left a flower and creepy note on her bed. All the doors and windows were secure when she arrived. Police are on their way now, but with so much time having passed and a contaminated crime scene, it's going to be difficult finding any evidence, let alone the culprit."

"Any potential suspects?" Bear was all business.

"Possibly. Name is Stanley Paulson. Former

foster brother who hasn't been heard from in a couple years, but would randomly show up out of the blue while she was at college and leave her letters. Obsessed with her for years and expected they were going to be married even though they didn't have that kind of relationship. Last known location was St. Louis. She mentioned his name yesterday, but I haven't had time to run a security check on him."

"What's your eighty-six?"

I slowed briefly before passing a slow moving vehicle and then sped up again.

"En route to the house now. ETA ten minutes."

"Call me back when you get there and the police have been appraised of what's going on. In the meantime, I'm going to talk to Hank and see if we can get more intel on this Paulson guy."

I relaxed the tiniest bit knowing I had the aid of the Brotherhood Protectors. We all might not be in the war anymore, but we still had each other's backs.

"Thanks, Bear. I'll be in touch."

"Roger that."

I ended the call right as I reached the edge of town, which forced me to slow my speed a notch. Frustrated that I couldn't go faster, I wound my way through Bitter Rock until I finally reached

Evie's neighborhood. Five turns later, I was on her street and pulling in front of the house behind a police car. A cop stopped me at the door, a hand raised.

"I'm sorry, sir, but you can't come in."

"Sebastian!"

Evie pushed past the officer and collided against my chest. She was shaking.

"Are you okay?"

She nodded against my chest. "I am now that you're here. Thank you for coming."

"I told you I'm here whenever you need me."

I tucked her against my side and stepped past the officer into the house. Paul was seated on the couch, his hair rumpled like he'd been running his hands through it.

"What have the police said?"

Paul rubbed his hands on his thighs. "Nothing yet. They only arrived shortly before you did. Evie explained what she'd found, and they've been upstairs since. We were told to wait down here."

Any further conversation was interrupted by footsteps coming down the stairs. Two suit-clad men appeared. The older gentleman, who led the two, paused for a heartbeat when he spotted me.

"And you are?"

I rose from the couch with my hand outstretched.

"Sebastian Nichols."

He shook it in greeting. "Detective Striker, and my partner, Detective Lang."

I received an imperceptible nod from his younger partner, but otherwise was ignored.

Evie jumped in. "Sebastian is my friend . He's the one who said we needed to call you."

"I'm a private contractor for a security and protection agency based out of Eagle Rock."

Striker pulled out a notebook and pen. "Does this security agency have a name?"

If this wasn't about Evie's safety, I'd take offense at his tone. "It's called Brotherhood Protectors. Owner is Hank Patterson."

The detective wrote down the info and turned to Evie. "Our team is still processing the scene, but we need to ask you a few questions."

"Of course."

"So you said when you arrived home last night you found both the letter and the flower on your bed. Is that correct?"

"Yes."

"Where were you?"

Evie's eyes darted in her father's direction and a

blush crossed her cheeks. "I'd had dinner with Sebastian and we'd gone back to his house."

Striker scribbled on his pad. The quiet one, Lang, asked the next question.

"What time did you arrive home?"

She paused to think about it for a moment. "It was a little before eleven."

"The doors were locked when you arrived?"

"Yes. As soon as I got home, I went upstairs. I spotted the items on my bed and went around the house and checked all the doors and windows. They were all secure."

Striker turned to Paul. "Where were you when your daughter came home?"

"I was asleep. I usually go to bed around nine-thirty."

He looked at Evie. "Why didn't you wake him up?"

She trembled and her expression shifted. "Honestly, I was really hoping he'd been the one to leave them there."

More scribbling. "Do you know anyone who might have left those things for you?"

She worried her lip and I held her hand. Her eyes caught mine and I nodded.

"There's a possibility it could be my former foster

brother. The minute I moved into the Paulson household, he was constantly underfoot. He would drive me to school even though he was several years older than me, and went to a different one. He'd invite me to go to the arcade with him and his buddies. I thought he was my friend so I'd go. Random things like that."

Both detectives suddenly seemed a lot more interested. "Can we get a name?"

"Stanley Paulson."

"Did he ever… behave inappropriately?"

Evie's forehead crinkled in puzzlement, but then she realized what Striker was asking. "Eww, no. He was just always there. Every time I turned around. Then there was Vanessa."

"What about her?" Paul chimed in.

"No offense daddy, but she was a bitch."

Her father and I both choked back a laugh.

"Who was Vanessa?" Lang asked.

She faced him and Striker. "She's the Paulson's daughter. She was two years older than me and hated me on sight. I have no idea why. I never did anything to her, but she treated me like dirt."

"What about Stanley and Vanessa? Were they close?"

She shrugged. "Not particularly. At least not that

I ever noticed. They seemed to have your typical older brother/younger sister relationship. The two of them fought on occasion, but nothing out of the ordinary."

"And you haven't heard from anyone in the Paulson family since you've lived here?"

"Nothing."

Needing to touch her, I reached for her hand.

There was silence as the detective consulted his notepad. After a minute, his gaze returned to Evie.

"Aside from this Paulson, is there anyone else who might have done this? Any co-workers maybe?"

She shook her head. "I've only taught at Bitter Rock Junior High for a couple years. I'm cordial with all my co-workers, but none have seemed overly interested in me."

"What about any of your students? Any of them seem to take an exorbitant amount of interest in you?"

"Not to my knowledge. None of them stick around after class to talk to me. I haven't seen them loitering around either before or after school either. None of them have given any indication that they have a crush. At least not in an obvious way."

Striker rose and pocketed his notebook before pulling out a business card and handing it to Evie.

"I think that's all the questions we have for you for now. If you think of anything or if another incident happens, give me a call. In the meantime, the evidence team should be finishing up in a couple hours. Please don't venture outside this room until they finish processing the entire house, except to the bathroom. We'll be in touch."

We all shook hands and the gentleman left. Paul paced, and I sat on the couch, pulling Evie back down with me.

"I talked to my boss. We're good at what we do, and I have the resources for assistance with security if we need it. In the meantime, I think it would be best if we set up some type of surveillance around the house. Flood lights, cameras, alarm system, that sort of thing. Just as a precaution."

"Sebastian," she paused. "I can't afford what you're suggesting."

"Don't worry about that. It's taken care of."

I pressed a finger against her lip to stop her next flow of words. "Don't push me on this, Evie."

She let out a resigned sigh. "Fine."

CHAPTER 19

My stomach was in knots and I was worried about my food not staying where it was. I knew Sebastian could sense my tension, because he reached across the table and clasped my hand.

"Everything's going to be okay. We'll figure out who did this. I promise."

I clutched his hand like a lifeline.

"I don't know what I would have done without you. Thank you for being here."

"There's no place I'd rather be."

"Do you mind if we go to your house for a little bit? I can't be in mine right now."

He didn't seem surprised. "Anything you want."

We rode in silence. After he parked, he held my hand and led me inside.

"Do you want something to drink?" he asked from the kitchen.

Instead of answering, I pulled his head down and covered his lips with mine. I didn't want to think. I only wanted to forget.

"Evie?"

I knew what he was asking.

"For years I've played it safe. I've held myself back. I haven't lived. Now this? I'm tired of being scared. I don't want to be that person. The one who looks back on her life and wonders why she didn't do a single thing for her. I want you Sebastian."

He cupped my jaw, his thumb rubbing across my cheek.

"Evelyn, Evie, I know you're afraid. This isn't the kind of decision you want to make without really thinking it through."

I covered his hands with mine and stared up at him beseechingly. "I've thought about nothing else since I met you. Even when you were being a jerk, I was attracted to you. It was why it hurt so much that you didn't seem to like me. Which is dumb, but that's just how it is. I can't get you out of my head. I want this. I want *you*."

He continued to stare down at me, gauging my sincerity. I didn't flinch or shift from his appraisal.

"If you're sure."

"I'm positive. Please."

Finally, my plea reached him. Together we went upstairs and I got my first look at Sebastian's bedroom. Of any man's bedroom.

A perfectly-made bed graced one wall and a single chest rested at the foot. Next to the head of the bed was a nightstand, but other than that, the room was devoid of any other furnishings or decorations.

I didn't know what to do next. Sebastian must have sensed my hesitation because he turned me to him and threaded his fingers in my hair before leaning down to kiss me.

I circled his neck with my hands and pressed myself against him. Soon, I relaxed into the kiss, lashing my tongue against his. I wanted more. I moved my hands and placed them under his shirt hem. His flat stomach jerked at my touch. The heat of his skin scorched the tip of my fingers, and I absorbed the burning sensation. Still, it wasn't enough.

I tugged on his shirt and he helped me pull it up and over his head. My eyes were glued onto his perfect washboard abs I remembered from the day he and my father had been on the roof.

"You're beautiful," I stated with awe.

I swear a flush covered his cheeks. "I think I'm supposed to say that to you, not the other way around."

My hands were at his waistband working the button when Sebastian covered my hands with his.

"Not yet."

I felt chastised. "Oh, okay."

He lightly gripped my chin between his thumb and forefinger and smiled. "There's no rush."

Slowly, he repeated my actions and my shirt joined his on the floor. His eyes sparkled and his nostrils flared as he took me in. My nipples pebbled beneath my bra from a combination of arousal and cold.

"Beautiful doesn't even begin to describe you, Evie. Breathtaking. Stunning. Gorgeous."

No one had ever made me feel all those things before. Now, I felt a surge of power.

"Thank you for saying that."

"Every word is true."

I pulled him down for another kiss. Our hands roamed each other's bodies, learning the texture of our skin. Sebastian was hard where I was soft, his skin rougher in places. I'd never get tired of touching him. I poured every ounce of feeling I had into my kiss. If I didn't, I'd explode.

I hadn't realized we'd moved until the bed brushed against the back of my knees. I fell back against it and he followed, keeping his weight off me. Then he went right back to kissing me. Hands roamed, lips and tongues touched, breaths weaved together. I wanted to touch Sebastian everywhere.

Cold air brushed my breasts as he removed my bra. I arched into his hand when it covered my breast. His lips left mine and traced a path downward until he reached my other freed breast. The dual combination of mouth and hand had me gasping and an ache traveled straight to my core.

"Please," I moaned the word.

"Tell me what you need, Evie."

"Don't know. So heavy. Ache. Sebastian. Please."

I gasped when he cupped my sex through my pants. His hand was so hot, and the throbbing intensified.

"Do you need me to touch you here?" He emphasized his question with grating friction of his hand against my pussy.

"Yes, there."

Sebastian slid his hand down my waistband and I almost came out of my skin when his fingers brushed against me. Against my protest, he removed his hand.

"Lift up."

I did what he asked, and ever so slowly, he began to pull my pants down over my hips and finally off my ankles. He thumbed my panties and gave them a sharp tug.

"Again."

My hips rose again and finally, I was completely naked beneath Sebastian. His eyes roamed my body and an appreciate light entered his blue depths.

"Fuck, Evie. You make me lose my mind with lust. I hope you know that."

I couldn't help but giggle.

"The feeling is mutual. Sometimes I can't believe I can speak intelligently around you."

"Well, if you can speak by the time we're finished, then I need to work on my lovemaking skills."

Lord this man made me laugh. Suddenly his expression flattened into one more serious. He brushed my hair back off my face. His cobalt eyes stared down at me.

"Do you know you're the first woman I've made love to since Natalie? The first one to see how tore up my leg is."

He moved off me and unbuttoned his pants. In

fascination, I could only stare as he pulled them down leaving him in only his boxer briefs. I was torn between where to look first. His obvious erection or his prosthetic leg. He made it easy for me by reaching down and pressing a button or something on the side of his leg and pulling it off. He rolled down a squishy-looking sleeve to fully expose what was left of his leg.

Thick scarring covered his limb from mid-thigh down. My heart ached for the pain he must have been in. I glanced up to see Sebastian staring at me like he was gauging my reaction.

"I'm sorry for the pain you suffered. Not just your leg, but your heart."

He didn't answer. Instead he lowered himself and covered my lips with his. He continued kissing me until I forgot about anything else. Our tongues danced and my hands clutched at his shoulders. His strong hand engulfed my breast, giving it some much needed attention. My whole body was on fire with need. Sebastian trailed kisses down my body. I thought he was going to stop at my breasts, but he continued on. With slight pressure from his hands, my legs parted.

I sucked in air. He didn't stop, only continued the sensual assault. Licking. Nipping. Sucking. Before I knew it, I was lifting my pelvis upward needing more. When he pulled my clit into his mouth and sucked hard, I almost bucked him off—the sensation was too much. I writhed in ecstasy beneath him, and my naked body was soon damp with sweat. There was a slight twinge of pain and some pressure when he pressed a finger inside me.

I dug my fingers into Sebastian's scalp, but he didn't stop what he was doing. The tension inside expanded throughout my body and the knot in my core continued to grow waiting for the right moment to escape. I chased the feeling, and when he bit down on my clit, my orgasm exploded from me. Sparks flashed behind my eyes and my body shuddered and trembled while I cried out his name.

He scooted up and pulled me against him, holding me close against his chest. Even in my relaxed state where my brain wasn't working quite yet, I kept waiting for more. That couldn't be all. I mean, we hadn't… he hadn't.

"I wasn't thinking straight, Evie. I don't have a condom."

"I'm a virgin, and you haven't been with anyone in years, right? I'm on the pill too." In my post-orgasmic bliss, I blurted it out.

His whole body froze.

"Evie," his voice was cautious.

I'd already gone this far. There was no turning back now.

"I want everything you have to give me. No holding back."

He hesitated only briefly before kissing me. Since I was still in bliss, it didn't take long to get ramped up again. Not with the way Sebastian was touching me. Needing to touch him as well, I slid my hand down his stomach and stopped at his waistband. It wasn't virginal reservations that held me back from exploring further. It was the fear that I wanted to please him as much as he pleased me, and I didn't know how to go about it.

"You can touch me anywhere you want, any way you want. Nothing you can do is wrong."

Taking that as my cue, I continued my exploration. Not feeling bold enough yet to slide my fingers under the elastic, I caressed his length through the fabric. Hard heat. Those were the two thoughts that came to mind. It was like caressing steel. I stroked Sebastian a few more times, but his hand covered mine, halting the movement.

"This will be over before it starts if you keep that up."

A surge of power rushed through me that I could

make this man lose control. It was a heady feeling. My eyes locked on his movements when he reached down and lowered his boxer briefs. His cock sprung free and my gaze locked in on it. *Holy crap.* I had no idea how that thing was going to fit, but I knew we'd make it work.

Hesitantly, I reached out and touched it. My finger traced the vein from root to crown and circled the purplish head. A small drop of wetness leaked from the tip and I dragged my fingertip across it before smearing it around. I glanced up at Sebastian. His eyes were hooded and his teeth clenched.

"Is this okay?" I whispered.

"God, yes," he hissed, his voice guttural.

I stroked him up and down a few times loving the velvet heat beneath my fingers. A pout graced my face when he stopped me once again.

"No more. I want to make this good for you."

"You already have," I assured him.

"Then I want to make it better."

He leaned down and I automatically opened my lips to greet him. Sebastian moved over my body to rub his cock up and down my slit, wetting his length and butting up against my clit with each stroke. I shuddered, the tension gently coiling again.

I gasped when he entered me, and my body stretched to accommodate him. He pushed little by little and then stopped. I felt full, and the discomfort made me shift a bit.

"Keep going," I begged.

"I'm sorry. This is going to hurt."

With a single thrust, Sebastian fully seated himself inside me. It burned like hell-fire. He remained still above me, letting my body adjust to the sensation. Slowly the pinching pain diminished and I was left with a dull ache.

"I can't hold still much longer," he said behind gritted teeth.

Tentatively, I lifted my hips, and Sebastian groaned and counter-thrusted. His pelvis rubbed against my clit and a tiny tingle of pleasure shot through me.

"Again."

He repeated his movement, and I met him halfway. "I'm trying to be gentle, Evie."

I wrapped my ankles around his rear and tugged him down to me.

"I don't want gentle." I punctuated my words with another upward thrust as I pulled him toward me with my legs.

That was all it took. Sebastian began pushing in

and out in earnest, and I met him stroke for stroke. The sharp pain had fled and instead a minor twinge took its place. But none of that mattered, because the sensation of his fingers against my clit overrode it. The electric shock was too much and pleasure crested over me. For the second time, I called out Sebastian's name. Right behind me, he reached his release, my name bursting off his tongue.

Exhausted, he half collapsed on top of me. Instinctively, I unhooked my ankles and he rolled off, pulling me with him so I was half-splayed on top of him, my sweat slicked skin quickly cooling. I shivered with the cold. Sebastian tugged the covers over us and I cuddled against his warmth.

"Thank you."

He chuckled. "You're welcome."

My eyes grew heavy and a drowsy feeling spread through me. I scooted closer to Sebastian and laid my head on his shoulder with my arm slung over his chest. The pull of slumber was too much and I drifted off.

CHAPTER 20

EVIE STIRRED NEXT TO ME. After she'd fallen asleep, I'd crept out of bed and into the bathroom to wash off and put my boxers back on. Then I'd come back with a warm washcloth and washed her as well. She'd awakened briefly while I took care of her, but she'd gone right back to sleep. She needed the rest.

Her eyes fluttered opened before her gaze homed in on me. She smiled shyly, and a hint of pink dashed across her cheeks.

"Hey there," I greeted her.

"Hi. Sorry I fell asleep."

"Don't worry about it. I know you needed it."

"How long have I been out?" She brushed her hair back off her face.

"Not long. Maybe twenty or thirty minutes."

"I should probably get going. I don't want to leave my dad alone for much longer."

She started to rise. Knowing she was probably feeling a little shy, I dropped a kiss on her forehead.

"I'll be downstairs."

I quickly donned my prosthesis and headed to the kitchen. A short time later, I heard the creaking of the stairs and then Evie came around the corner. I handed her a bottle of water.

"Thanks."

"I'll take you home when you're ready."

"I just need to grab my purse."

∽

After I dropped Evie off, checked to make sure all was clear at her house, and she locked the door behind me, I set off back home where my computer was. I pulled up the drive and headed inside. While my laptop was booting up, I called Bear again.

"What's the sitrep?"

"Police came and went. Processed the scene and two detectives asked a bunch of questions. Seemed competent, but not necessarily motivated. What about on your end? Anything on Paulson?"

I quickly logged into my computer and tapped some keys while Bear spoke.

"Actually, yes. Got a hit on a purchase he made a couple weeks ago. One-way plane ticket to Bozeman. Arrived two days ago."

"That would have given him plenty of time to get to Bitter Rock."

"Damn, Nichols, what have you gotten yourself into out there?"

"I need to set up some home security for Evie's house. Alarm, cameras, the works. Take it out of my paycheck."

"Don't worry about that. I'm sending a guy out today. Should be there by morning. In the meantime, we don't know how dangerous this Paulson guy is, so watch your six. We already know he's in the area."

"Roger that. Thanks, Bear."

"You know we look after our own, Nichols. Take care, and I'll text you the guy's contact information."

"Thanks."

It took me about fifteen minutes, but I finally got a hit on the car. Rental out of the Bozeman airport to Stanley Paulson. I just needed to find out where he was now.

CHAPTER 21

A WIDE YAWN escaped before I could contain it. Sebastian and I had been spending the last few nights together, and I'd hardly gotten any sleep.

I sat at my desk grading the last few assignments, and it was well after five. I needed to finish them so I could head over to Sebastian's. I'd finally gotten my car back from the shop. My savings account was crying, but it was a relief having my own transportation again.

We were finalizing the plans for my dad's birthday party this weekend. It was hard to believe he was turning fifty. In my mind he would always be in his mid-30s, even though I saw the graying hair and the age lines sprouting from the corners of his eyes every day. Even with those minor signs of aging, my father was still a handsome man, and I could see what my mother saw in him as a young man.

Finally, I finished writing the last B+ at the top of the paper and capped my red pen. I slid the papers and my pen into my shoulder bag, and headed out of my classroom, locking the door behind me. Shelby had poked her head in about ten minutes ago to say goodbye, so other than the janitor, who was somewhere in the building, I was the last one here.

The sky was dark and cloudy when I stepped outside, and I hoped it wasn't going to rain before I got to Sebastian's. I picked up my pace, my head down, when I felt the first droplet of water on my cheek. Crap.

I reached my car, and my fingers had touched the door handle when I heard a noise behind me.

"Hello, Evelyn."

My heart dropped in my chest, then raced wildly, while every other muscle froze. I forced myself to start breathing again and my muscles to relax. Right as I began to turn, a surprisingly strong arm wrapped tightly around my waist, and a sweet smell invaded my nose. I attempted to scream when a cloth covered my face. I struggled against the vice-like grip and clawed at the hand while the panicked sensation of my oxygen being cut off grew. I continued thrashing as I felt myself being dragged backward. Briefly, the fabric was removed and I was being jostled, but before I could take a deep breath, it was back in place.

My surroundings weaved in and out of focus. Before I could guess what was happening, I was pulled into a vehicle, still securely pressed against the man's hard chest. My vision blurred and my entire body went languid and pliant.

"That's right Evelyn, stop fighting. Just relax. We're together now."

~

My arm tingled. I attempted to reposition it, but I couldn't move my hands. My eyes flew open and I struggled. I glanced around the room in terror and discovered I was in a motel room, laying uncomfortably on my side, my hands tied behind my back. I tried to roll, but the rope around my ankles halted my movement.

"I see you're awake. I was beginning to worry I'd used too much chloroform."

My head jerked up at the masculine voice. I locked eyes with the man standing against the door, arms crossed over his chest. He'd changed over the last two years. He was still only average height, but before, his body had been spindly and wiry, and he now had muscle.

"Stanley." My voice cracked.

He uncrossed his arms and pushed off the wall. His steps were fluid and unhurried. He squatted . I flinched when Stanley reached out to brush my hair out of my face. He crossed his forearms and laid them on the bed.

"You've been a naughty girl, Evelyn."

His eyes glowed with an unhealthy light. They fastened on me in a way that sent a shiver through me.

"What are you doing, Stanley? Untie me."

His lips pressed together and his expression hardened like stone. "You don't give the orders around here, Evelyn. I can't believe you'd betray me like this."

He quickly stood and began to pace around the small room. I quickly processed his words, but they made no sense to me.

"Betray you? What are you talking about? Please, untie me. My fingers are numb."

Stanley moved behind me. I winced at the pulling and tugging, but finally my hands were free.

"The legs stay tied."

I twisted and maneuvered and was finally able to sit myself up on the edge of the bed. I rubbed my wrists and hissed at the pins and needles sensation.

"Thank you, Stanley."

I wanted to stay on his good side.

"The first time I saw you, I knew you were meant for me. You came into our house as this lost little girl, yet never once did I see you cry. You were too strong for that. Even Vanessa couldn't break your spirit, although I know she certainly tried. That's when I knew."

His eyes grew unfocused and his expression distant like he was remembering that time. My gaze darted around the room searching for a weapon. Anything I could use to get out of here. There was nothing.

"I watched you grow from that young girl into a woman. You watched me too. It didn't matter that I was five years older than you. I could tell you had feelings for me, no matter how hard you tried to hide them. I knew. It was in the way you talked to me. The way you would blush when I smiled and then you'd return my smile with one of your own. It was shy, but sweet. Every time I came home from college, you were always there, waiting for me."

I could only stare. Nothing he said was true. I'd avoided him at all costs and never had I given him the impression I was into him. Holy shit, he really was bat shit crazy.

"I let you go to school and get your fancy teaching degree, and this is how you repay me? By going behind my back and screwing some nobody? You are mine, Evelyn." Spittle shot from his mouth as he spat out those last four words.

Terror had me still as a statue, afraid to move and ignite Stanley's fury any more. He was unstable, and a wrong move on my part was a disaster waiting to happen. I tried making my words conciliatory.

"I'm sorry, Stanley."

He either didn't care about my apology or he was so far gone in his rage that he was deaf to anything I said.

"I saw the way he was pawing at you at his house. No one is allowed to touch your body but me, Evelyn."

The first night at Sebastian's when we'd heard the crash outside his house.

"That was you?"

Stanley smirked, pleased with himself. "If I'd had a baseball bat with me that night, I would have solved my little problem then."

Bile rose in my throat.

"In fact, I might still do that. Your Sebastian won't be so handsome anymore by the time I'm through with him."

An insane glaze covered Stanley's eyes while he strode back and forth across the stained carpet of the run-down motel room he'd holed us up in... wherever we were. I didn't know what to do other than pray Sebastian was safe.

CHAPTER 22

A QUICK GLANCE at the clock confirmed Evie was late. I'd lost track of time while I'd been outside.

My phone rang and I gave a sigh of relief. There she was. Evie must have got tied up at school and hadn't been able to call. My brow crinkled though when the unknown number flashed across the screen.

"Hello?"

"Oh my god, Sebastian? I think something happened to Evie." The woman's voice was rushed and shrill.

Alarm filled me. "What? Who is this?"

"This is Shelby Davis. I work with Evie. She'd been working a little late and I'd just left, but I'd forgotten some papers on my desk that I needed so I turned around and headed back. I pulled into the parking lot and a black car was parked next to Evie's clunker. It started driving away. They passed me, and I didn't see her in the passenger seat, but there was a man driving. Something just felt off."

"How long ago?" I barked out.

"I don't know, maybe thirty minutes. I called the police, but they didn't seem to care. Then I called Evie's house and talked to her dad. He told me to call you."

I fired up my computer.

"Did you happen to get a license plate?"

"I did actually. One of the things my father taught me was to get a plate."

Shelby rattled off the number and I jotted it down while I waited for my computer to boot up.

"Anything else you can tell me. Did you get a look at the driver?"

She sighed heavily. "The windows were tinted pretty dark, so I couldn't get a clear view. I know it was a man, and I'm pretty sure he had short, dark hair. Unfortunately, that's all I can tell you."

Frustrated I couldn't get more info, but knowing it wasn't her fault, I thanked her. "If you think of anything else, call me immediately."

"I will."

I ran another trace on his banking information and prayed I found some additional credit card activity that would indicate his location. So far, I'd had zero luck, so I assumed beyond the rental car, he'd been using cash.

I needed to call Paul. He had to be worried sick about Evie.

"Have you heard anything?"

"Nothing yet, I'm sorry. I'm working on getting the license plate of Stanley's rental and matching it with the number Shelby gave me from the car she spotted leaving the parking lot. I'm also trying to track down any credit activity as we speak. Until then, there's nothing else I can do."

"I can't just sit here and do nothing."

"I know it's hard Paul, but until I get a hit on something, I'm in the same boat. I'll let you know the minute I find something. I promise."

Ten minutes later, I hit paydirt. I called Paul.

"I got a hit. Paulson used his credit card at a hotel about halfway between here and Bozeman earlier today. My guess is that's where he's headed. I'm getting in my truck now and I'm going to head out there."

"I'm coming with you."

"No," I bit out, then softened my tone. "I don't

know anything about this guy, especially whether or not he's armed. If he does have Evie, I can't be worried about both of you. I need you to stay here. I'll let you know when I find her. In the meantime, call Detectives Striker and Lang. Let them know what's going on. Give them my number and have them call me."

Paul took in a shuddering breath. "She's all I have, Sebastian."

"I know. I'll bring her home."

I disconnected our call and jogged into my office. Jerking open the file cabinet drawer, I lifted the lockbox out and flipped the numbers on the combination lock until the correct sequence showed. I quickly grabbed my 9mm and a magazine before rushing out to my truck. Plugging in the address of the hotel into my GPS, I tore down the drive and prayed.

CHAPTER 23

STANLEY HAD TIED me back up and gagged me before saying he had to run an errand quick. The minute he stepped out of the motel room, I'd been doing everything I could to get free. My wrists were wet and I knew I was bleeding. My right arm was killing me, but that was my own fault for falling off the bed and onto the floor. I didn't care. I was desperate to escape.

My entire body froze when the doorknob rattled and clicked. Survival instincts kicked into action, because I started screaming behind the gag, praying it was housekeeping coming in. My yells were abruptly cut off when, instead of a housekeeper, it was Vanessa who stepped through the door.

She smiled so evilly a shiver raced through me, and now I wanted to struggle for a different reason.

"Well, well, well, look who we have here."

She stepped into the room and shut the door behind her. She moved forward, almost slithering across the room.

"Miss high and mighty seems to have been dropped down a peg or two. Not so uppity now, are ya?"

She obviously didn't expect an answer. Her eyes glared with a hatred I still didn't understand.

"My brother is still an idiot over you I see. How pathetic." She rolled her eyes. "Personally, I never knew what the big deal was. Still don't."

Instinctively, I flinched when Vanessa reached forward, but she merely removed the gag from my mouth.

"Thanks," I croaked out through dry lips.

We continued to stare at each other. She made no move to release my bonds.

"Why do you hate me so much?" I should be asking her to untie me.

She sneered. "Do you have any idea what it was like, day after day, hearing about how amazing your father was? And to watch Stanley pant after you too? Your dad went to prison for you. My dad couldn't even be bothered to look up from his newspaper. I wasn't important enough to have a five-minute conversation with."

Vanessa rose, and I used every muscle I could to sit myself up and prop against the dresser. Warily, I watched as she paced back and forth across the room.

"Your dad wrote you letter after letter. You talked to him weekly on the phone. All I ever got was silence. I could handle that, because I had Stanley. He kept me company, talked to me, hung out with me. Then *you* showed up and it was like I didn't even exist anymore."—I almost felt sorry for her, but there was a maniacal look in her eye that had me nervous. None of it was my fault.

"I'm sorry you were hurting Vanessa. But you and I both know that I never once encouraged Stanley."

"It doesn't matter," she spat. "You were the only thing he cared about. Still are the only thing he cares about. But I'm here to solve that little problem."

Dread spread through my gut and a queasy feeling followed. "Wha—what are you talking about?"

Instead of answering, she opened her purse and pulled out a gun. *Oh my god.*

"Once you're out of the way, Stanley will forget

all about you. He'll need me, his sister, to help him through his grief. He'll finally pay attention to me."

"Vanessa," my voice trembled. "You don't want to do this. Please. It won't change anything. I'm sorry, please."

She raised the gun.

"Vanessa, please," I begged.

The door behind her opened and she swung around, her gun now pointed at the intruder.

"Stanley," I called out.

His eyes zeroed in on Vanessa.

"Van, what are you doing here? And what's with the fucking gun?"

She waved it crazily at him, her finger not on the trigger, but too close for comfort.

"For years, you and Dad ignored me, never acknowledging me. And it's all because of *her!*" Her free hand pointed in my general direction.

"Good god, Vanessa, give me that damn thing before you shoot someone."

"Like her, you mean?"

Stanley held out his hand in a coaxing manner. "Everything is going to be okay. Just hand me the gun."

"No." She stomped her foot. "She has to go, Stanley."

Before I could even blink, he dove for the weapon in her hands. They wrestled for control, and I jerked when the gun went off. The echo was deafening, and then silence reigned. My eyes darted between the two when Vanessa pulled away. Stanley remained standing, a glazed look in his eyes, his hand pressed against his side. Blood poured around his hand, covering it in blood before dripping onto the floor. His eyes were wide, his mouth forming words that didn't emerge.

He fell to his knees, still clutching his side, and then he crumpled to the floor. Vanessa spun around to me her eyes wild with shock.

"Look what you made me do."

"Call 9-1-1. Get help."

She wasn't listening.

"This is all your fault," she cried out. "You made me do this. You killed him."

There was a loud crash behind her, and the door slammed open.

"Drop the weapon!"

My heart raced when I saw Sebastian standing there with a gun. Everything that happened next was a blur. Vanessa turned and raised her gun in his direction. I screamed when a shot rang out. Sirens blared, and I could only watch in horror as Vanessa stumbled and fell, landing in a heap alongside her brother.

"Evie," Sebastian yelled and raced over to me.

I hissed in pain as he untied me. Everything hurt when he pulled me to my feet and wrapped me in his arms.

"Police!"

We both turned as Detectives Striker and Lang entered the room with guns drawn. They took in the scene and tentatively lowered their weapons as they approached the brother-sister pair. Striker rolled Vanessa over and checked for a pulse. He looked up at us and shook his head. Stanley groaned when Lang moved him.

"Shit, he's alive."

"Ambulance is on the way."

Sebastian led me to the bed and I sat down, my legs giving out just as I made it over there.

"Are you okay? Are you hurt anywhere?"

I clutched his hand in mine and I never wanted to let go. "I'm fine. Just shook up."

Striker approached us.

"Ms. Vincent, we're going to need a statement from you."

Evie nodded. "Yes, of course."

"Can you please come by the station first thing

tomorrow morning? I'm sure you want to get home and get some rest."

"Yes, please. I'll be there bright and early."

He tilted his head at Sebastian who pulled me up from the bed, wrapped his arms around me, and escorted me out to his truck. Once he'd secured me safely inside, we headed for home. I jumped when a phone appeared in my periphery.

"We need to let your dad know you're okay."

Oh god, how could I have forgot about my father?

His frantic voice almost had me in tears.

"I'm okay Daddy, I swear. I was worried too. I love you. I'm with Sebastian right now. We're heading back to town. We'll see you soon."

I set the phone on the seat between us and the stress from the last few hours hit me and I burst into tears. Quickly, Sebastian pulled off to the side of the road and slid across the seat to wrap his arms around me. I clung tightly to him and sobbed against his chest.

"I've never been so scared in all my life. I thought she was going to kill me."

"Cry it out, baby. You're okay now. No one is going to hurt you. I'm here."

I continued bawling until I had no tears left. I

sniffed a final one back and pulled away to wipe my eyes.

"I'm sorry."

He lifted my chin with two fingers so I had to look him in the eye.

"Don't ever be sorry. If you weren't crying after all you've been through today, I would be worried about you."

"How did you find me?"

Sebastian pulled back onto the road.

"I tracked Stanley to this location and prayed you were with him."

"Vanessa is dead?" I hated the relief I felt at that.

"Yes. If Stanley makes it, he'll be going to prison for a long time."

I couldn't find it in my heart to care. All of this was his fault. Utterly exhausted, I rested my head against the window. Sebastian held my hand in his the whole drive home and let me sit in blissful silence.

When we pulled into my driveway, my father rushed out the door like he'd been watching out the window for us to arrive. I burst into tears again when he hugged me tight.

"I'm so glad you're home. I was so scared. I love you, Evie girl."

"I love you too, Daddy."

The three of us went inside and I sat on the couch with my dad. Sebastian disappeared down the hallway, but quickly returned with a first aid kit. He knelt at my feet.

"Let's get those wrists taken care of."

Gently, he doctored my wrists with antibacterial ointment and wrapped some gauze around them.

"I need to get in touch with Bear. Will you be okay if I head home for the night? I can come pick you up in the morning and take you to the station."

"Will you stay? Please?"

"If that's what you want, of course I will."

I clutched his hand. "I don't think I can sleep by myself."

"I'm here for you, Evie."

My father stood and kissed the top of my head. "You two go on. I'll clean up down here and then I'm going to head to bed myself."

I stood and hugged him hard. "Thank you, Daddy."

"Get some rest. I'll see you in the morning."

Sebastian and I went upstairs to my room. I undressed. He followed suit, and once his leg was off, we both crawled into bed. I reached over and shut off the bedside light before rolling over and plastering myself to his side.

"Hold me."

He wrapped his arm around me and pulled me tighter against him. "Always."

I let out a shuddering breath and closed my eyes, praying for sleep.

CHAPTER 24

It had been a month since Evie was kidnapped. Stanley had recovered from his gunshot wound, but had taken his sister's death surprisingly hard. Currently, he was in the county jail after being charged with kidnapping and various other felony charges. He'd been denied bail. Thankfully, I'd been cleared of any charges regarding Vanessa's death. They ruled it self-defense.

We'd celebrated Paul's fiftieth birthday with a small, intimate party with just the three of us. But when we'd gone out to dinner, we'd run into her friend Shelby, Shelby's boyfriend Ryan, and Ryan's mother, Sheila. They'd invited us to join them.

Apparently Paul and Sheila had hit it off, because they'd been spending a lot of time together since that night. Which was probably a good thing, since Evie had been spending most nights with me. She was having the occasional nightmare. Any time she had one, I pulled her close and held her until it was over. Most nights she didn't remember them.

I was sitting in my office when Evie walked through the front door after work.

"Hey, how was school today?"

She dropped her messenger bag onto the side table and kicked off her shoes before dropping onto the couch in a tired heap.

"Lord, what a day. Finally, after months and months of trying, I actually got through to one of my students and she opened up to me about all the trouble she's been having at home and school. The things she told me, Sebastian, just make me want to cry. I knew she was having difficulties, but not to this degree."

I sat down on the couch and lifted her feet onto my lap. She moaned in pleasure as I rubbed and massaged the soles of them.

"That feels amazing, thank you."

"You're welcome. I'm glad she has you to talk to and go to bat for her. There's no doubt you're a wonderful ally for her to have."

She sighed. "I'm just glad she trusts me. Now I have to keep it."

"I have no doubt you've done and will continue to do everything in your power to help her."

"Thank you for your confidence. How was your day? Any new cases?"

I must have hit a particular spot, because Evie practically melted into the couch. I smiled that I could get my woman to relax that easily.

"Bear has a couple for me, local ones, especially now that I'm staying here permanently."

"You and my dad have done so much amazing work around this place. It's really come together. You're going to make the sexiest rancher in Montana." She winked at me.

I threw my head back. "Maybe in Bitter Rock."

"Well, *I* think you're the sexiest rancher in the whole state."

I quickly moved out from under her legs to on top of her, caging her beneath my body.

"Your opinion is really the only one that counts."

I brushed my lips across hers and she sighed into them. I stared down at her and my heart expanded. I knew how I felt about Evie, but I'd been keeping a lock on it. I couldn't do it any longer. A worry line appeared between her brows.

"Sebastian? You okay?"

"I love you."

She blinked. And blinked again as tears filled her eyes and a small smile crossed her lips.

"I love you, too."

Her fingers threaded through my hair and she pulled me down to her. Our passion quickly rose and before I knew it we were tearing off our clothes. I didn't even take the time to doff my prosthesis before I was lining my cock up against her pussy and thrusting home. Our movements were guided more by desire than finesse. I reached between us and found her clit. A few flicks and thrusts later, Evie climaxed, her body shuddering beneath mine. I thrust a couple more times and I followed right behind her.

Trying to keep most of my weight off her, I half-collapsed against her. My prosthesis twisted and I cringed at the ache it sent through my limb. My cock slipped out of her, and I needed to stand and move from the awkward position my leg was in.

"Oh dear, is your leg okay?" Evie sat up and reached out to massage my thigh. She'd done that ever since the night I'd told her I still get the occasion muscle spasm.

"I'm good, babe. Just needed to stand. Come on, let's go get cleaned up and change our clothes."

We walked to the bathroom and quickly showered. Sadly, shower sex was out for us, because I didn't want to take any chances of slipping or losing my balance and dragging Evie down with me if I fell. We dressed and headed downstairs for dinner.

"I'll clean up in here. You go out in the living room and relax." I picked our dishes up and started to wash them.

"Let me help."

With soapy hands I handed her the glass of wine she hadn't finished yet and gently pushed her out of the kitchen. "I got it. Go. Relax. That's an order."

Evie smartly saluted me and I popped her on the ass. She giggled and rubbed the spot. "Fine."

After I was finished, I opened the cupboard above the stove. It was empty and too high for Evie to reach anyway. I pulled down a small box. Opening it, I gave it a long glance before closing it again and shoving it in my pocket. Then I followed Evie out into the living room.

She was sitting on the couch with her legs tucked underneath her and some soft jazz playing on the stereo while she sipped the rest of her wine. I didn't realize my hands were shaking until I slipped the glass from her fingers and set it on the side table.

Evie must have sensed my nervousness. "Is everything okay?"

"Hmm," I mumbled. "Oh, yeah, it's fine."

I took both her hands in mine.

"From the day I met you, there was this spark to you. It only gets brighter every day. When Stanley took you, I almost went mad with rage. And fear. I'd lost one woman I loved already. I'd be damned if I lost another."

Evie's eyes grew damp. "Oh, Sebastian. You won't lose me."

I released one of her hands and dug into my pocket. She gasped when I held my palm open. Tentatively, she reached out for it, her eyes darting back and forth between mine and the box. I covered her hands with mine and together we opened the package.

Tears that had been gathering spilled over her lids. Secured between satin covered cardboard was a platinum engagement ring with a single carat princess cut diamond in the center. It suited Evie perfectly. I lifted the ring out and set the box aside.

I reached for her hand and slid the ring on her third finger. "After Natalie died, I didn't think I'd ever find love again. Until I met you. I've been given a second chance. You saved me, Evie. Saved me from a life of loneliness. I wasn't really living until I met you. I want to spend the rest of my life with you. I love you Evelyn Elise Vincent. Will you marry me?"

She nodded and threw her arms around me. "Yes. God, yes. I love you so much."

I hugged her close and knew that I would do everything in my power to make this woman happy for the rest of our lives.

ORIGINAL BROTHERHOOD PROTECTORS SERIES

BY ELLE JAMES

Brotherhood Protectors Series

Montana SEAL (#1)

Bride Protector SEAL (#2)

Montana D-Force (#3)

Cowboy D-Force (#4)

Montana Ranger (#5)

Montana Dog Soldier (#6)

Montana SEAL Daddy (#7)

Montana Ranger's Wedding Vow (#8)

Montana SEAL Undercover Daddy (#9)

Cape Cod SEAL Rescue (#10)

Montana SEAL Friendly Fire (#11)

Montana SEAL's Mail-Order Bride (#12)

Montana Rescue (Sleeper SEAL)

Hot SEAL Salty Dog (SEALs in Paradise)

Brotherhood Protectors Vol 1

ABOUT ELLE JAMES

ELLE JAMES also writing as MYLA JACKSON is a *New York Times* and *USA Today* Bestselling author of books including cowboys, intrigues and paranormal adventures that keep her readers on the edges of their seats. With over eighty works in a variety of sub-genres and lengths she has published with Harlequin, Samhain, Ellora's Cave, Kensington, Cleis Press, and Avon. When she's not at her computer, she's traveling, snow skiing, boating, or riding her ATV, dreaming up new stories. Learn more about Elle James at www.ellejames.com

Website | Facebook | Twitter | GoodReads | Newsletter | BookBub | Amazon

Follow Elle!
www.ellejames.com
ellejames@ellejames.com

facebook.com/ellejamesauthor
twitter.com/ElleJamesAuthor

Made in the USA
San Bernardino, CA
31 October 2019